Willow's Wood

"Have all the dogs been walked?" said Bob.

"All done," said Bev. "But I have to—"

"Dad!" Neil interrupted. The mention of dog walking had reminded him of what had happened that afternoon. "We won't be able to walk the dogs for much longer. Not on the ridgeway."

"What do you mean?" Bob asked.

"They're going to dig it all up," said Emily, flaring up. "It's going to be ruined."

Everyone stood still and paid attention.

"Yes," Neil said. "They're going to use the land to build a road."

Titles in the Puppy Patrol *series*

More Puppy Patrol stories follow soon

Puppy Patrol
Willow's Wood

Jenny Dale

Illustrated by

Mick Reid

A Working Partners Book

MACMILLAN CHILDREN'S BOOKS

Special thanks to Cherith Baldry

First published 2000 by Macmillan Children's Books
a division of Macmillan Publishers Limited
25 Eccleston Place, London SW1W 9NF
Basingstoke and Oxford
www.macmillan.co.uk

Associated companies throughout the world

Created by Working Partners Limited
London W6 0QT

ISBN 0 330 39090 2

1 3 5 7 9 8 6 4 2

A CIP catalogue record for this book is available from
the British Library.

Typeset in Bookman Old Style by SX Composing DTP, Rayleigh, Essex
Printed and bound in Great Britain by Mackays of Chatham plc, Kent

Chapter One

"Here, Jake! Fetch!" Neil Parker hurled the small branch he had been holding and watched as his young black-and-white Border collie bounded after it through the grass on top of the ridgeway.

The sun was starting to set. Wind ruffled Neil's spiky brown hair as he looked down towards the small country town of Compton in the distance. Much nearer he could see his home, King Street Kennels, where his parents, Bob and Carole Parker, ran a boarding kennels and rescue centre.

The ridgeway, on the far side of the Parkers' exercise field, was perfect for walking the dogs.

Eleven-year-old Neil couldn't think of anything he enjoyed more than being up here with Jake.

"This is one of the best places in the world," he said.

His younger sister Emily didn't reply. She was crouched down with her backpack dumped beside her, peering into a clump of longer grass and scribbling something on the clipboard she held.

"Coltsfoot!" she said triumphantly. "That's my twentieth flower."

Neil groaned. Just lately, Emily had talked about nothing but the project Mrs Rowntree, her teacher, had dreamed up. All the class had to identify wild plants and flowers and make notes of how they changed during the Easter holiday. Neil was glad that he didn't have to do it, but Emily was enthusiastic. She loved lists and the project meant making lots of them.

Neil turned away as Jake came dashing up with the branch between his jaws. "Good boy!" he said, holding his hand out. "Give!"

Jake let him take the branch, and then stood waiting excitedly for Neil to throw it again. Neil was pleased with him; not long ago Jake had wanted to play tug-of-war with anything Neil threw for him, but now he was learning to obey Neil's command.

Neil bent down and ruffled Jake's glossy fur. Jake's jaws were wide in a doggy grin as he panted eagerly. His eyes were bright and alert. Looking at him, Neil couldn't help remembering Sam, Jake's dad, who had died rescuing his young puppy from drowning. Neil never stopped missing Sam, and he was determined to do all he could to make sure that Jake grew into a fit and healthy dog.

Neil fished in his pocket for one of the dog treats he always carried, and gave it to Jake. Then he threw the branch again. "Fetch, boy! Go fetch it!"

Jake tore off and disappeared into the undergrowth on the edge of a stretch of woodland that covered that part of the ridgeway.

"Let's follow Jake," said Emily. "There'll be lots of different flowers under the trees."

"OK," Neil said. Jake could search for interesting new smells in the wood while Emily worked on her project.

Neil's sister stooped down beside a huge tree and began to examine a fungus growing on the roots. Neil watched as she fumbled in her backpack for the field guide that helped her identify new finds.

Jake had vanished, but Neil could still hear his happy barks and the rustling sound he made as he plunged through piles of dead leaves.

Then he heard another sound: the heavy footsteps of someone making their way through the trees. Half expecting another dog walker, Neil looked up to see a tall, dark-haired man in an orange jacket tramping through the bracken and brambles.

The man hadn't seen Neil or Emily, but as he came closer Jake bounced up to him, leaping around wildly with the piece of wood in his mouth. The man barely glanced at Jake. He didn't try to take the branch, or play with him; he just ploughed on through the wood, looking angry.

"Jake!" Neil called. "Here, boy!"

Jake didn't seem to hear him. He bounded after the man and leaped up playfully at him. The man swung his arm in a violent swiping motion, but missed.

Jake thought it was all a wonderful new game. He dropped the branch, and sprang up for the man's arm.

By now Neil was running towards them. "No, Jake!" he yelled. "Down, boy! Sit!"

The man backed away from Jake, and aimed

a kick at him. Jake growled playfully and caught hold of the side of the man's boot with his teeth.

"Jake!" Neil yelled.

Since puppyhood, Jake had always loved worrying feet. He would never hurt anyone, but the stranger didn't know that. The man jerked his leg, dislodging the young Border collie, as Neil dashed up and grabbed his dog by the collar.

"Sit, Jake," he said sternly.

Jake gave him a look, as if he couldn't understand why Neil sounded so annoyed. Then he sat obediently. Neil straightened up, out of breath, and faced the man.

"Sorry," said Neil. "He was only playing."

"That's a dangerous dog." The man sounded furious. "And he's out of control. You're not fit to be in charge of him."

"Oh, come on . . ." said Neil.

"He bit me."

Neil peered at the man's foot. There were a few marks where Jake's teeth had been, but it was a stout boot, and the man couldn't have been hurt.

"He thought it was a game," Neil tried to explain. "You shouldn't have waved your arm at him."

"Oh, so now it's my fault, is it?"

The man gave Neil an unfriendly stare. He was big and heavy, stocky rather than over-weight, and his dark hair was starting to go grey. Like Emily, he was carrying a clipboard. Neil wondered what he was doing up on the ridgeway.

"I've said I'm sorry," he repeated. "Jake's not vicious."

"He's really friendly." Emily came up and squatted down to put an arm round the Border collie. Jake, who was sitting panting, turned his head and gave her a swipe across the face with his tongue. "Look, you can see he is."

The man snorted. "What if I reported you to the police? What about that, hey?"

Neil shrugged. He couldn't take the threat seriously. Sergeant Moorhead, the head of Compton's small police force, knew the Parkers and Jake well. No one would ever persuade him that Jake was dangerous.

"If you want to bring the dog up here you should have him on a lead," the man went on.

"Eh?" Neil couldn't believe what he was hearing. "We bring him here so he can have a run. Dogs need proper exercise, you know." He patted Jake. "Anyway, we're going now," he said. "I'm sorry if Jake frightened you, but he wouldn't have bitten you, honestly."

The man let out another snort, as if he was offended that Neil thought he had been frightened. He began to stride away, and turned back to say, "Make the most of it. You won't be giving him a run up here for much longer."

Neil and Emily stared at each other. "What do you mean?" Neil called.

But the man was already making his way out of the wood. Neil dashed after him, with Jake trotting alongside and Emily just behind.

They caught up with him at the edge of the trees. A second man was there, collecting up tools that lay scattered around a noticeboard.

"Have you finished?" the first man asked. The other grunted in reply. "Let's be going, then."

Neil stood and confronted him. "What do you mean, we won't be giving our dogs a run up here for much longer?"

The man looked from Neil to Emily with a satisfied expression on his face. "I'm the chief transport engineer for Compton Council," he said. "You won't be walking your dogs here, because this wood won't be here – or the rest of this site."

"Site?" said Emily. "What site?"

Both men started walking away, down the hill. The transport engineer looked back, and called over his shoulder, "Read the notice!"

Neil and Emily walked around the notice-board to see what was on it.

"Oh, no!" Emily exclaimed.

Neil gasped with shock. The notice was headed:

PROPOSED ROUTE
COMPTON BYPASS

*

Neil flung open the door and dashed into the kitchen at King Street Kennels. "Mum! Dad!"

He stopped as he realized that the kitchen

was unusually crowded. As well as Neil's mum and dad, and his five-year-old sister Sarah, Kate and Bev, the two kennel-maids, were there, and Kate's boyfriend Glen Paget. For some reason everyone was looking happy. Bob Parker was opening a bottle of wine.

As soon as Neil appeared in the doorway, Sarah rushed over and grabbed him. "Neil! Neil! Kate and Glen are getting married!"

"What?" Neil spluttered. For a minute the bad news about the bypass went out of his head. "That's great!"

Glen was a student at Padsham Agricultural

College, and the Parkers had always expected that he and Kate would wait to get married until after he had finished his course and found a job.

Kate looked pink and excited, and her eyes were shining. She held out her hand to Neil and Emily to show them a sparkly diamond ring. Glen was grinning widely.

"We decided to bring it forward," he explained, "because my mum's boss is going to Brussels for two years, and he's asked Mum to go with him as his PA. She doesn't want to miss helping out with the wedding, and we don't want to wait that long until she gets back."

Bob poured out the wine and handed the glasses round, and Neil fetched orange juice from the fridge for himself, Emily and Sarah.

"I know you'll both be very happy," Bob said, "and we all want to wish you good luck. Let's drink to Kate and Glen!"

"Kate and Glen!" everyone chorused, and drank the toast.

Neil gave Jake a titbit so his dog didn't feel left out.

"So when *is* the wedding?" Neil asked.

"Three weeks tomorrow," Glen told him. "We went to see Gavin Thorpe at the Parish Church yesterday, and it's all fixed."

"That doesn't give you long to get ready," said Carole.

"Yes, there's so much to do!" Kate said. "I don't even know where we'll have the reception yet."

"Well, you'll have the reception here, of course," said Carole. "In the barn."

"Oh, that would be marvellous!" said Kate. "Are you sure? It'll be a lot of work."

"I shall enjoy the challenge," said Carole.

"And I'll help," said Bev.

Emily added, "So will I. We all will. It'll be a real Puppy Patrol wedding."

"Oh, Kate!" Sarah said, jumping up and down. "Can I be a bridesmaid? Can I, please?"

"Of course you can," Kate said. "I haven't any little brothers or sisters, so I wouldn't have a bridesmaid at all if it wasn't for you. You too, Emily."

Sarah beamed, and Emily nodded, looking pleased.

"And Neil can be a pageboy," said Glen with a wicked grin. "In a velvet suit."

Neil shuddered. "No way!" Jake woofed in agreement.

Bob drained his glass of wine. "Well, this

11

won't get the work done," he said. "Have all the dogs been walked?"

"All done," said Bev. "But I have to—"

"Dad!" Neil interrupted. The mention of dog walking had reminded him of what had happened that afternoon. "We won't be able to walk the dogs for much longer. Not on the ridgeway."

"What do you mean?" Bob asked.

"They're going to dig it all up," said Emily, flaring up. "It's going to be ruined."

Everyone stood still and paid attention.

"Yes," Neil said. "They're going to use the land to build a road."

Chapter Two

"What?" said Carole.

"They're going to cut through the ridgeway to build the Compton Bypass," Neil confirmed.

"They can't really do that, can they?" Emily said. "We've got to stop them!"

"Calm down," Bob said. "And tell us about it properly."

Neil sat at the kitchen table. Everyone gathered round to listen as Neil and Emily told the story of their meeting with the chief transport engineer.

"He was horrible!" said Emily. "Who needs a stupid road anyway?"

"Now hold on," said Bob. "The traffic in

13

Compton town centre is pretty bad."

"You can hardly breathe for petrol fumes sometimes," Carole added.

"A new road would help that, and ease congestion in Colshaw and Padsham as well," said Bob.

"Dad, you don't mean you want the ridgeway spoilt?" Neil asked.

"I didn't say that," Bob replied, tugging thoughtfully at his curly brown beard. "I think a road is needed. But I don't understand why they want to build it there. It's not just our dog walking. The ridgeway is an important area for wildlife, and if they put a road through it they'll have to cut down trees that have stood for centuries."

"If they took the road round the other side of Compton," Carole said, "there wouldn't be nearly so much damage."

"So why aren't they?" asked Neil.

Bob shook his head. "Beats me."

"But there must be something we can do!" said Emily. "Glen, you know about this sort of thing. What do you think?"

Glen frowned, thinking. "But I do know somebody who might help. If I can use your phone, Bob, I'll give her a ring right away."

14

"Help yourself," Bob said.

Glen went out.

"We could organize a petition," Emily said. "Or a march . . ."

"Plenty of people would support it," said Kate. She got up to fetch the latest issue of the *Compton News*, which had been delivered earlier that day. "Let's check in the paper."

She spread the newspaper out on the table, and everyone leaned over to look as she turned the first page. Jake hopped up on to a chair so that he could look, too.

"Here we are," Kate said. "Second page. *Much needed new road for Compton area.* And there's a map of the route it's going to take."

Neil peered at the map. It only gave a rough outline, but it was clear that miles of the ridgeway would be affected. "They can't *do* this," he said.

Bob got up, and came back a minute later with the local Ordnance Survey map. "Look," he said, spreading it out. "They'll be taking a chunk out of Old Mill Farm—"

"Wow! It'll be that close!" said Neil.

"That's going to please Jane and Richard," said Bev sarcastically.

Jane and Richard Hammond owned the

neighbouring Old Mill Farm. They were good friends of the Parkers and Jane's dog, Delilah, was Jake's mum.

"What about the exercise field?" Emily asked.

Bob traced the line of the new road with one finger. "No, that won't be touched," he said. "But we'll have lorries whizzing by on the other side of the hedge. And then – look – they'll be taking a couple of fields off the edge of Priorsfield Farm. Harry Grey will be *livid*."

"But that's OK," Neil said, thinking he saw an easy solution. "Jane and Richard won't let them build a road on their land. Neither will Harry."

Bob shook his head. "It doesn't work like that, Neil. Landowners can be forced to sell, if the land is needed for something else."

"But that's not fair!" Emily exclaimed.

"It's the law, I'm afraid," said Carole.

The kitchen door opened and Glen came back in. He was grinning; Neil thought he must have good news.

"I spoke to my friend Liz Hart," he said. "She's really into environmental protest, and she thinks this is something her group would definitely be interested in supporting. She's going to find out what she can, and then get back to me."

16

"That's great!" said Neil.

"I'll let you know as soon as I hear from her," Glen said. "But now I'd better take Kate home. We've got a lot to do!"

When Kate and Glen had said goodbye, the Parkers looked at the newspaper again. There were a lot of traffic statistics in the article, and details of pollution from cars going through the town centre, to show how much the road was needed. But there was nothing about the damage it would cause.

"We could start by writing a letter to the paper," Carole suggested. "There's going to be a lot of local protest about this."

"There's bound to be a public enquiry," said Bob. "And if—"

The phone rang in the office, and he stopped what he was saying to go and answer it.

"I can't *believe* this," Neil said, tracing the route on the map again. "It'll change everything."

Carole nodded. "It's not just the road itself. It's the noise, and the pollution."

"And once it's built, it's built," Emily said gloomily. "The ridgeway will be ruined."

"It's *not* going to be built," said Neil. "Not if we can help it."

Carole started to fold up the map and the

17

newspaper ready to serve supper. Neil and Emily were setting the table when Bob came back in. Neil thought his dad looked as if he had something on his mind. "Who was that on the phone, Dad?" he asked.

"Last-minute booking," said Bob.

"Anyone we know?" Carole asked, as she took baked potatoes out of the oven.

"Guess." Bob grinned reluctantly. "Who are our *favourite* boarders ever?"

Emily's mouth dropped open. "Oh, no! Not Sugar and Spice!"

"The very same."

"But I thought Sugar and Spice went to Pretty Paws now," Neil objected.

Pretty Paws dog hotel in Colshaw wasn't just a kennels – it was a doggy beauty parlour for very pampered pets. That sort of thing was just what Sugar and Spice's owners, the Jepsons, liked best, and their two Westies were the most spoilt dogs in the whole of Compton.

"Apparently Pretty Paws is full," Bob explained. "Mrs Jepson isn't well, Mr Jepson tells me, so next week she's going off for a few days to Happydale Health Farm."

"Where?" Neil said, while Emily exploded into giggles.

"It's somewhere over the other side of Compton," Carole said. "I've heard you just spend all day being massaged and drinking lemon juice. If Mrs Jepson would take those dogs for a good walk regularly, it would be better for all of them, and she wouldn't need a health farm." She set a dish of cauliflower cheese on the table. "Right, supper's ready."

When everyone was sitting down, Bob said, "That's not all. After I'd taken the booking, I asked Mr Jepson about the new road. He's on the council, so I thought he might know something. And he was very odd about it."

"You mean odder than usual?" Neil asked.

"He just said he couldn't discuss confidential council business, and put the phone down."

"I don't see what's so confidential when it's in the paper," said Carole.

"Oh well." Bob shrugged. "I'll try again next week, when they drop off their little darlings."

"Can't wait," Neil mumbled.

There was no more news over the weekend. On Monday afternoon, Neil and Emily cycled into Compton to talk to Gavin Thorpe, the vicar, about borrowing tables and chairs from the church hall for Kate and Glen's wedding

19

reception. When they got back, Carole called them into the office.

"I've just spoken to Glen," she said. "He tells me that his friend Liz is very keen to help. This road is exactly the sort of development that she and her group are fighting against."

"So what's she going to do?" Neil asked.

"It's what she's already done that counts," said Carole, smiling. "According to Glen, she says the most important thing is to get the protest moving quickly, and not wait for a public enquiry to be organized. So she and some of her friends have set up camp on the ridgeway, where the road will go through. She says they're going to stay there until the plan is dropped."

"You mean they're up there now?" Emily said, eyes wide with amazement.

"That's right."

"Then what are we waiting for?" said Neil.

As Neil and Emily were crossing the courtyard, with Jake at their heels, they saw Kate coming out of the storeroom with a broom.

"We're going up on the ridgeway," Neil said. "Mum says there's a protest group camping up there. Do you want to come with us?"

"No thanks." Kate waved the broom. "Far too much to do!"

They said goodbye, and set off across the exercise field and on to the ridgeway.

It was another sunny day. Jake ran ahead, barking excitedly, pushing his nose into every hollow and clump of grass.

"Look at him!" said Neil. "Just think, one day we might not be able to bring dogs up here again . . ."

"No," said Emily determinedly. "Don't think about that yet. What we've got to think about is how to stop the road."

Neil watched as Jake disappeared at the top of the slope. He could still hear him barking, and after a minute a second dog joined in.

"They've got a dog up there!" said Neil.

He put on speed to get to the top of the ridgeway. Further along the track, at the edge of the wood near the site notice, a cluster of tents had been pitched. Three or four people were squatting around a camping stove.

That wasn't what interested Neil though. Close by, Jake was playing with another dog – a small, scruffy white dog who was running in circles around him, leaping and letting out flurries of happy barks.

Emily laughed. "Jake's found a friend!"

Neil wasn't so pleased. Even though he

enjoyed the sight of Jake and his new friend getting to know each other, he couldn't help worrying about what was best for the little dog.

"Is that their dog?" he asked, gesturing towards the group of tents.

"How do I know?" said Emily.

"If it is and they're living up here, can they really look after it properly?" Neil said. "I'm going to sort this out." He strode determinedly up to the tents. Jake followed him, and the little white dog scampered happily alongside.

Emily shrugged her shoulders and followed her brother.

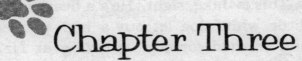

Chapter Three

As Neil drew nearer to the group around the camping stove, a girl of about Kate's age got to her feet. She was tall and striking-looking, with long dark hair hanging loose. She wore denim jeans and a bright blue sweater.

"Hi!" she said. "You must be Neil and Emily Parker."

Neil was so surprised that he forgot he had meant to ask about the white dog. "How do you know?" he asked.

The girl laughed. "Glen told me about you. I'm his friend Liz." She bent down and held out a hand to Jake, who trotted up and sniffed her fingers interestedly. "He told me about your

23

dog, too. This is Jake, right? He's a beauty."

The little white dog let out a high-pitched bark, and pushed forward, nuzzling at Liz's hand. Liz rumpled the curly white hair on the top of the dog's head. "OK, I haven't forgotten you, girl," she said.

"Is she yours?" Neil asked.

"That's right. Meet Willow."

"Hi there, Willow," said Emily.

Neil pulled a dog treat out of his pocket, and held it out to Willow, who slurped it up from the palm of his hand. Jake came and nosed at Neil's pocket, as if he was asking, "What about me?"

Neil fished out another titbit for him and asked Liz, "Is it good for Willow, living on a campsite like this? Can you look after her properly up here?"

Liz looked surprised, and Neil wondered if she was going to be annoyed with him. Even if she was, he didn't feel sorry for asking the question. He had to be sure that Willow was well looked after.

Then Liz smiled. "I can see you care about dogs," she said. "But there's no problem, honestly. Do you want to come and see?"

Neil nodded. "Sure."

Liz led the way over to one of the tents.

"Willow loves running around the camp," she said. "She knows not to stray too far. And I give her a good walk every day." She lifted the flap of the tent. "This is where we sleep, and I keep her food in here."

Inside the tent a sleeping bag was stretched out, and beside it was a plastic dog basket with a cosy blanket inside. A wooden crate held packets of all-in-one dog food and dog biscuits, as well as several bottles of water. A bowl of water stood on the ground beside the crate; Willow stuck her nose into it and lapped noisily.

"I don't just give her the all-in-one food," Liz explained. "I buy tinned food or fresh meat, for variety."

"She looks really bright and healthy," Emily said admiringly.

"She is," said Liz. "I check her over every day, and I groom her so she doesn't get burs and stuff in her coat. And if we're here for very long I'll make sure she gets a check-up from the local vet."

"That's Mike Turner," Neil told her. "He's great. I know he'll help if you have a problem."

"Brilliant," said Liz. "I'll show you something else, too. Hey, Willow – trees!"

Willow had finished her drink. When Liz

25

spoke to her she pricked up her ears and trotted out of the tent as far as one of the trees which stood a few metres inside the wood near the campsite. It was old and gnarled, with its trunk growing at an angle. Just above head-height, a few planks were lashed securely to the branches to make a platform.

"This is where we go if they try to move us off the site," Liz explained. "Once we're settled in, we'll build some more. They can't cut the trees down if there are people in them."

"Great idea!" said Emily.

"Now watch this," said Liz. "OK, girl, up you go!"

"But dogs can't—" Neil began.

He broke off. Willow scrabbled with her front paws at a knothole in the slanting tree trunk. She hauled herself upwards with her back paws working furiously, and managed to climb up to where the trunk forked. From there she scrambled along a sloping branch until she was underneath the planks. Barking excitedly, she hopped up a couple of side branches that made a convenient ladder, launched herself up on to the platform and sat looking over the edge.

"Forget I spoke," Neil said feebly.

Liz laughed, and Willow sat with her tongue

lolling out as if she was sharing the joke. "It's her party trick," Liz said. "She loves climbing trees. I can't keep her on solid ground!"

"That's *so* clever!" said Emily.

Jake had put his forepaws up on the trunk of the tree and looked up to where Willow was sitting. He whined softly.

"Oh, no!" Neil said. "*You're* not going up there!"

"How does she get down?" Emily asked.

"Like this." Liz slapped her leg. "Come on, girl! Down!"

Willow gave her a look as if she wanted to say, "I like it here!" Then she stepped off the edge of the platform on to the nearest branch and half slid, half jumped down to the ground again. Jake sniffed at her as if he couldn't believe what she'd just done, and then the two dogs dashed off into the wood, scuffling together happily.

Neil grinned as he watched them go; he loved to see dogs playing together. He guessed that Willow must be about the same age as Jake, and the two young dogs looked like becoming real friends.

He left them to their game and walked back to the camp with Liz and Emily.

"So you're in charge of organizing this camp?" Emily said. "Do you really think you can stop them building the road?"

"We'll have a good try," Liz said. "We've stopped developments in other places. One of the most important things is to get local protest off the ground really quickly. Let the council know that it can't do whatever it likes and spoil the countryside for everyone else in the process."

"We'll help," said Emily.

"Sure we will," said Neil. "We can—"

Just then one of the men around the camping stove stood up, looking along the ridgeway, and said, "Hey, Liz, we've got company."

Neil glanced over to where a figure was walking purposefully towards them. The newcomer was a tall young man with his hair drawn back into a ponytail. He carried a camera, and wore a baggy denim jacket.

"That's Jake Fielding," said Neil. "He's a reporter with the *Compton News*."

"Then he's just the person I want to talk to," said Liz.

She strode along the track to introduce herself to the young photographer and bring him back to the camp with her.

When he saw Neil and Emily he gave them a friendly grin. "Hi there. I've just been talking to your mum and dad. They gave me a lot of good reasons why this road shouldn't be built."

"I bet they did," Neil said. "It would mean a lot of changes for the dogs round here."

Jake pulled out his reporter's notebook. "So tell me, Ms Hart, what's the thinking behind this protest?"

"Call me Liz. The main point is that there's another route, on the other side of Compton, that would be just as good, and wouldn't destroy nearly as much beautiful scenery and wildlife. So why is the council choosing to dig up the ridgeway?"

Jake was scribbling. "I'm told the other route would be more expensive to build."

"Not that much more expensive," Liz retorted. "Besides, the construction cost isn't the only important thing. What about the cost to the environment?"

Neil was impressed. He could see that Liz had really done her homework, even in the short time that she'd known about the road plan.

"And what would you say about—" Jake was beginning, when the two dogs shot out of the wood again, chasing each other and barking madly.

"Jake," said Neil, talking to the reporter, not his dog, "you should meet Willow. She's the best protester of the lot!"

"Willow?" said Jake Fielding. "That's the dog, right?"

"Right," said Liz.

"She climbs trees!" said Emily. "That would make a great picture!"

"Climbs trees?" Jake grinned and reached for his camera. "Now this I've got to see!"

Liz whistled for Willow, and led the reporter over to the tree with the platform. Neil and

Emily were about to follow, when they heard someone else calling their names.

Jane Hammond, with her black-and-white Border collie Delilah, had appeared at the top of the slope. Jane was small, with dark curly hair. She wore a padded jacket over a sweater and corduroy trousers.

Delilah ran off to say hello to her son Jake, while Jane stood looking around. "So this is the protest camp," she said. "There aren't many people here, are there?"

"I think this is just the beginning," said Neil.

"We've got to get lots more local support," Emily added.

"Well, you shouldn't find that difficult," Jane said. She looked annoyed. "We had a letter from the council this morning to say that they've applied for a Compulsory Purchase Order for part of our land. That means we have to sell to them, whether we want to or not."

"Oh, no!" said Emily.

"Richard rang Harry Grey at Priorsfield Farm," said Jane. "He's had one, too." She was still gazing down the hill towards her own fields and the Parkers' land. "I don't understand why the council picked this route," she went on. "Who made the decision? And why can't they see that the other route would be so much better?"

"We should *make* them all come up here," said Emily. "Then they'd see what they're going to spoil."

"Not so easily done, though," Jane said. "But what we *can* do is make sure they know how everybody else feels about it." She shoved her hands deep into the pockets of her padded jacket, and stood there looking obstinate. "By the time they set up the public inquiry, we need to have the whole of Compton up in arms!"

"I've been thinking," said Neil.

He and Emily were on their way home; they had left Jake Fielding taking pictures of Willow in her tree, and Jane Hammond telling him about the Compulsory Purchase Orders.

"What about?" Emily asked.

"The stuff Jane said," Neil explained. "*Why* are the council so keen to use the ridgeway route? If we knew that, it might help us to stop them."

"Good idea," said Emily, "but how do we find out? Councillor Jepson wouldn't tell Dad anything."

"Then let's ask somebody else," said Neil. "I

thought we might go and see Marjorie Foster."

"She's not on the council," Emily objected.

"She always knows what's going on, though," said Neil.

Marjorie Foster worked as a legal clerk for a Compton firm of solicitors, White and Marbeck. She was grateful to the Parkers for their help when her father's dog, Skye, had been accused of sheep worrying, and since then she had often given them advice.

"It's worth a try," Emily said thoughtfully, and then with enthusiasm, "Let's go for it!"

The next morning Carole asked Neil and Emily to start cleaning up Red's Barn ready for the wedding, so they had no time to visit Marjorie Foster until the afternoon. As they got off their bikes in Compton's market square, they saw her coming out of the offices of White and Marbeck.

Emily waved, and Neil called out, "Hi, Mrs Foster!" He left his bike with his sister and pounded across the square; Emily followed when she had padlocked the bikes to the railings of Queen Victoria's statue.

Marjorie Foster was smiling as they came up. She was a slim, middle-aged woman with brown hair, and she wore a smart navy blue business suit.

"Mrs Foster!" Neil panted. "We've got to talk to you!"

"Will it take long?" Marjorie Foster asked. "I've got a hair appointment."

"We'll walk with you," said Neil.

With Neil on one side of Marjorie Foster, and Emily on the other, they walked along the High Street. Neil had to admit that the traffic congestion was bad. There were queues of cars waiting at the pedestrian crossing, and it was hard to make himself heard over the noise of engines and horns.

"It's about the new road," he began. "They're going to build it along the ridgeway, so we won't be able to take the dogs up there any more."

"And it'll go right along the bottom of our exercise field!" Emily added.

"I can see that would be a problem," said Mrs Foster. "I don't like the idea either. It's going to pass the gardens at the Grange – you remember, the old people's home where my father lives? The noise will be terrible."

"So why do they want to do it?" Neil asked.

"Why indeed?" said Mrs Foster. "The whole of Compton will be against it. My boss, George

Marbeck, is organizing a local action group."

"What I'd like to know," said Neil, "is who chose the ridgeway. Who picked that route and not the other one?"

They had reached the hairdresser's; Marjorie Foster stopped. "You mean you don't know?" she asked. "I thought Councillor Jepson was a friend of your father's?"

"Not exactly," Neil explained. "He boards his dogs with us."

"Do you mean Mr Jepson is involved with the road?" Emily asked.

"You could say that." Marjorie Foster gave them a tight smile. "I heard about this from George, who's on the council. Please don't tell anyone that I told you."

"Right," said Neil.

"Well, then . . . A lot of the councillors didn't like the idea of spoiling the ridgeway, but quite a few were worried about the extra expense of the other route. When it came to the vote, the council was evenly divided. It just so happened that your friend Mr Jepson had the casting vote." She paused, and looked from Neil to Emily and back again. "*He* voted to build the new road across the ridgeway."

Chapter Four

The following morning, when the Jepsons' car drew up outside King Street Kennels, Neil was waiting. He stood by the gate while Bob said hello to Mr Jepson, and Mrs Jepson tried to coax Sugar and Spice out of the car.

Mr Jepson was tall and bony, and he hardly ever smiled. Mrs Jepson was plump, with frizzy blonde hair. Today she was wearing a frilly yellow dress with matching high-heeled shoes.

Sugar had decided that she liked it in the car, and refused to move. Mrs Jepson reached into the back, her dress straining at the seams as she bent over. "Come along, sweetie-pie," she cooed. "Come to Mummykins!"

Neil didn't know whether to laugh or be sick, but he stopped himself from doing either. Mrs Jepson straightened up clasping Sugar, who was slurping her tongue over her owner's face, smudging her make-up.

Spice scrambled out into the drive and started rolling over and over.

"Naughty baby," Mrs Jepson scolded. "Baby will get all dirty."

Neil thought that a bit of honest dirt wouldn't do either dog any harm at all. Their white fur was fluffed up, and they wore collars set with glittery stones, and matching ribbons on top of

their heads – pink for Sugar, blue for Spice. He couldn't understand people who treated dogs like the Jepsons treated their two Westies.

"I hear you're not well, Mrs Jepson," Bob Parker said. "I hope you'll feel better soon."

Mrs Jepson rolled her eyes upwards and patted herself on the chest. "It's my nerves, Mr Parker," she said. "I have such trouble with my nerves! Norman says it's because I'm too sensitive. Don't you, Norman?"

Mr Jepson grunted.

"So I'm going for a few days to Happydale Health Farm," Mrs Jepson went on. "Dr Upton, who runs it, is just wonderful! He understands my case very well. The only problem is, he won't let me take my babies with me."

Can't say I blame him, Neil thought.

Mr Jepson produced the vaccination certificates for the two Westies, and gave them to Bob. Mrs Jepson handed Sugar to Neil.

"Now you will take care of my darling doggy-woggies?" she said. "You know how much they love their choccies."

"Yes, we know all about that," said Bob. "They'll be well looked after while they're here. I promise."

"Mrs Sparrow at Pretty Paws always gives

38

them a shampoo and set," Mrs Jepson said. "I don't suppose you could . . ."

"I'm sorry," said Bob. "We really don't have the facilities for that here."

Mrs Jepson pouted. "Never mind, my darlings," she said. "You shall have a lovely shampoo next time."

She kissed both dogs on the end of their noses, and got into the car. Bob said goodbye, took Sugar from Neil, and managed to persuade Spice to follow him through the side gate.

As Mr Jepson was about to get into the driver's seat, Neil stepped forward. "Mr Jepson, I wanted to ask you about the new road."

Mr Jepson gave him an unfriendly look. "That's council business, as I told your father."

Neil took a breath. He was pretty sure that what he was going to say wouldn't make him popular. "Is it true that you chose the ridgeway route?"

Mr Jepson froze with his hand on the car door. He was frowning. "Where did you hear that?"

Neil shrugged. "Oh . . . around. I just wanted to ask why. Can't you see that—"

"Never mind why," Mr Jepson said. His voice rose. "How I vote in Council is my business. I suggest you mind yours, young man."

He got into the car and slammed the door. Neil stood watching as he drove away. He wasn't surprised that Mr Jepson had refused to discuss the road with him. But he felt he had learnt something. He had the definite impression that Mr Jepson didn't want to admit why he had chosen to support the route over the ridgeway.

The *Compton News* on Friday had a big spread about the protest group, with pictures of Liz Hart, and Willow up her tree.

Emily laughed when she saw it. "She's such an amazing dog!" she said.

"She's brilliant," Neil agreed. "I vote for going up there now, and paying her another visit."

"OK," said Emily. "I'll bring my class project. And why don't we take some of the boarding dogs with us? Only *not* Sugar and Spice!"

"Sugar and Spice would never make it up there," Neil agreed.

When Neil and Emily went out they met Bev crossing the courtyard with a couple of brooms.

"We're going up to the camp," Neil announced. "Do you want us to take some of the dogs?"

"It would be a help," said Bev. "Can you manage Cass, that Labrador in Kennel Block One? And the Irish setter a couple of pens further down? They're both big dogs, and they need a good run."

"No problem," said Neil.

Inside Kennel Block One Neil and Emily found Kate, delivering bowls of fresh water. Neil unfastened the door of Cass's pen, and unhooked the lead which hung outside it. Emily went to fetch the Irish setter, Paddy.

"Have you finished, Kate?" Neil asked. "Are you coming up to the ridgeway?"

Kate put down the last bowl and came out of the pen. She said, "No," and went out without stopping.

Neil stared after her. It wasn't like Kate to be so short with him. She didn't look like her usual cheerful self, either.

"What's wrong with her?" he whispered.

"I don't know," said Emily, clipping on Paddy's lead. "She wouldn't come last time we asked her, either."

When Neil had whistled for Jake, he and Emily set off to the camp. The little group of tents they had seen on their first visit had grown, and a line of them now spread all along the edge of the wood. There were many more people sitting around, and as Neil and Emily drew closer they could hear someone playing a guitar.

Then Jake gave a welcoming bark, and they saw Willow racing along the path towards them.

Neil couldn't help thinking how much Willow looked like Sugar and Spice. He would have bet that there was some Westie in her. But Willow was a proper dog, fit and healthy, and well-trained.

"Look!" said Emily, as Neil squatted down to greet Willow and give her a titbit. "There's Jake Fielding again. And isn't that Tony Bradley from the local radio station? This protest is starting to be really *big* news."

She headed off with Paddy to say hello to Jake Fielding, leaving Neil to follow more slowly. Cass, the Labrador, was a dog who liked to take her time.

As Neil passed the first tent, someone poked his head out. Jake burst into excited barking, and flung himself forward.

"Jake!" Neil shouted, and then realized that he needn't worry.

The person Jake was greeting so enthusiastically was Glen. "Hi, Neil," he said, grabbing Jake and rolling him over on the grass. The young Border collie waved his paws happily in the air. "Is Kate with you?"

"No," Neil said. He wondered whether to tell Glen about Kate's strange behaviour but decided not to. "I think she was too busy. Are you staying up here now?"

"Yes – at least till the college term starts. Liz needs all the support she can get."

"Did you see the picture of Willow in the *Compton News*?" Neil asked.

Glen laughed. "Yes. Willow's a great little dog." He clicked his fingers at Willow, who was lying on the turf close by, her jaws wide as she panted. "You know we're talking about you, don't you, girl?"

Just then Cass gave a huge yawn, and planted herself solidly on Neil's foot.

"I think this one's had enough," Neil said with a grin. "I'd better take her back, if I can drag Em away."

"Tell Kate I'll see her later," Glen said, and retreated into his tent.

When Neil found Emily she was talking to Toby Sparrow and Julie Baker from her class, who had come up to work on their project and see what was happening in the camp. They had

their heads together over their clipboards, comparing notes.

"You know we've got Sugar and Spice again?" Neil said to Toby. Toby's mum ran Pretty Paws dog hotel. "You're lucky you were full."

"We're not," said Toby. He grinned at Neil and lowered his voice. "Mum told Mr Jepson that if his dogs ripped up their pen again she would have to put an extra charge on their bill. Mr Jepson wasn't pleased."

Emily collapsed in giggles as Neil said, "I'll bet!"

"I wonder if Mrs Jepson knows?" Emily asked as she and Neil set off down the hill. "I think she'd pay anything for her little doggie-woggies to have their shampoo and set!"

Neil felt a grin spread across his face. "What if we threatened to tell her? Maybe we could get Mr Jepson to change his mind about the road."

"Neil Parker, that's blackmail!" Emily said, shocked. "It's *wrong*. Anyway, it would never work."

"No," Neil agreed reluctantly. "It's not important enough. All the same, there's something about that road he doesn't want people to know. You didn't see him, but I did, and he looked dead guilty."

"I wonder why," Emily said.

"I don't know," said Neil. "But I'm going to find out!"

When they had put away the boarding dogs, Neil and Emily came out of Kennel Block One to see Bev crossing the courtyard. She sighed exaggeratedly, but there was a twinkle in her eye.

"I've just cleaned those pens. And the dogs will mess them up again in seconds. It never stops, does it?"

"Nope, never," said Neil. "Is Kate around?"

"I think she's in the rescue centre. Is it important?"

"Just that I saw Glen up at the camp. He said he'd be down to see her later."

Bev frowned.

"Is something the matter?" Emily asked. "Kate was really strange before we left."

Bev folded her arms across her chest. In a low voice, she said, "Kate told me that Liz used to be Glen's girlfriend, long before he met Kate. I think she's upset that he's spending so much time up at the camp with her."

Neil and Emily exchanged a glance.

"But Glen is supposed to be marrying Kate," said Emily.

"That's why she's upset."

Neil sighed and bent down to scratch Jake's head. Having a great doggy friend like Jake was a lot simpler than getting married.

"Is there anything we can do to help?" Emily asked.

"I doubt it," said Bev. "And I don't think you should mention it unless Kate talks about it first. This is something that she and Glen will have to work out for themselves."

Chapter Five

"School starts again on Wednesday," Emily announced at breakfast the following Monday morning.

"Tell me about it!" Neil groaned.

"I haven't got nearly enough stuff for my project," his sister said, reaching for the marmalade. "And I phoned Julie and Toby last night. Julie can't come, but I'm going to meet Toby up on the ridgeway so we can work together."

"I'll come with you," Neil said. "To give Jake a run," he added – just in case Emily might think he was going to help her hunt for flowers. "And to see what's happening in the protest camp."

Jake sat up in his basket, and then bounded

across the kitchen to sit beside Neil's chair, thumping his tail on the floor. Neil slipped him the last piece of his breakfast sausage.

"I wish we could get Kate to come," said Emily. "Then she might feel better."

"We had a long talk yesterday," said Carole. She started to clear the plates and take them over to the sink.

"What did she say?" asked Neil. "Is she OK?"

"The real trouble is," said Carole, "Glen's spending all his time up at the camp now, and he isn't seeing much of Kate at all. Kate thinks it's because of Liz."

"Oh, that's stupid!" said Emily. "It's because Glen cares about the ridgeway, that's all. He thinks it's really important to stop the road."

"Stupid, hmm?" Carole said. "I'll remind you of those words, Emily Parker, in six or seven years' time when you have boyfriend trouble."

Emily grimaced.

"But Kate can't really think that Glen likes Liz best?" Neil asked. "I mean . . . well, Kate's Kate."

"You know Kate hasn't got much confidence in herself," said Carole. "Remember when Bev first came – Kate nearly gave up her job here because she thought Bev was so much better with the dogs. And now she thinks Liz is much prettier and cleverer than she is, and involved with all the things Glen's interested in too."

"But they're supposed to be getting *married* a week on Saturday!" said Emily.

"I know," said Carole. She started running hot water into the sink, and squidged in washing-up liquid. "Honestly, I'd like to go up to the camp and shake that young man until his brain starts working! I know the road's important, but there's only one thing Glen should be interested in right now, and that's Kate."

Emily giggled. "You wouldn't really do that, would you, Mum?"

"No, more's the pity. But if they are going to call the wedding off, I wish they'd make their minds up," Carole said. "I've already got a freezer full of sausage rolls and quiches!"

Neil and Emily tried to persuade Kate to come up the ridgeway with them, but Kate just said she had too much work. She looked pale and her eyes were red, as if she had been crying.

There was nothing for it but leave her to get on with the kennel work, and go up the hill by themselves.

This was the first time they had been there in several days, and the camp was even bigger now. Platforms had appeared in several more trees. Neil and Emily noticed Liz and Glen standing under Willow's tree, talking together, while Willow looked down, bright-eyed, from her platform in the branches. Glen was pointing up at her, and laughing at something Liz said.

Watching, Neil thought perhaps it was a good thing Kate wasn't with them.

Toby Sparrow had already arrived, and was sitting cross-legged at the edge of the camp with his clipboard in front of him. His Dalmatian puppy, Scrap, was trying to push his nose in front of the pencil.

"Get off, Scrap!" Toby said, laughing. "You don't know how to draw!"

"There should be celandines and anemones in the woods by now," Emily announced, when she had said hello. "And bluebells starting to come through."

"Let's go and look," said Toby.

"In a minute," said Emily. "I want to make some notes first."

"Flowers!" said Neil, grinning. "Who needs 'em? Eh Jake?"

Emily and Toby were busy over their

clipboards, when Liz came hurrying up, with Willow trotting at her heels.

"Hang on to your hats, people," she said. "We've got company."

Emily straightened up and pushed back her dark hair. "Oh, no!" she said. "It's him again."

Neil looked to where Liz was pointing. Two men in orange jackets were climbing the slope towards them. Neil recognized the one in the lead – the transport engineer who had first told them about the new road.

"What does *he* want?" Neil asked.

"To make a nuisance of himself, I should think," Liz said grimly.

Neil could see she had met the transport engineer before. He whistled for Jake. The young Border collie came running over, and gave Neil an injured look as he clipped on the lead.

"Sorry, Jake," Neil said, slipping him a dog treat to make up for his lost freedom. "But I'm not risking any more trouble."

"Trouble?" Toby said anxiously, pulling out Scrap's lead.

"This guy can't stand dogs," Neil explained.

The transport engineer was panting as he toiled up the last few feet, and stood glaring at Liz while he got his breath back. The man with him gave the protesters an unfriendly stare and started scribbling on a clipboard.

Liz smiled and said, "Good morning, Mr Tyler."

When the transport chief was able to speak, he snapped, "You might not think it's good when you hear what I've come to say. I'm giving your lot notice to get off this land."

"This is common land, Mr Tyler," Liz replied. "We have a right to be here."

"Just as much right as you have," Neil added.

Mr Tyler ignored him. "This is local authority land," he continued. "I'm a representative of that authority and I'm asking you to leave."

"Sorry," said Liz. "No can do. We're staying."

She glanced at Glen and the other protesters, who were gathering round to listen. They murmured their agreement, and Glen said, "You can't make us go."

"Oh, can't I?" Mr Tyler snorted. "You're trespassing, and if you won't leave of your own accord I can get the police to remove you."

One or two of the protesters looked alarmed at the mention of the police.

"I don't think so," she said crisply. "You see, Mr Tyler, I know the law as well as you do, and probably better. The police can't remove us unless we damage the land, or unless we threaten or insult the landowners or their employees. Well, we haven't damaged anything – we care for this land far more than you do. And we haven't threatened or insulted you, Mr Tyler." Her smile broadened. "However much we might like to."

Mr Tyler looked taken aback. His face grew red with anger. "It won't do you any good," he said. "This road is going to be built, whatever you do. It's what this area needs."

"In your opinion," said Liz.

"Some of us think that wildlife is more

important," Glen added. "Especially when there's another perfectly good route for the road that wouldn't do nearly as much harm."

"Never mind all that," the transport engineer blustered. "I'm giving you official notice to get off this land. In writing."

He pulled out a long brown envelope from his inside pocket and held it out to Liz.

Liz put her hands on her hips. "I'm not accepting that."

"Here, take it." Mr Tyler thrust the envelope at her, and when she still refused to take it, he dropped it at her feet.

"Litterbug!" someone said in the crowd.

Mr Tyler glared at them all and then spun round and stalked away, beckoning to his colleague to follow him.

"Hey, look at Willow!" said Toby Sparrow.

The little mongrel had let out a delighted bark, and seized the fallen envelope in her jaws. Then she trotted after Mr Tyler, as if she wanted to give it back to him.

"That's the idea, Willow!" Liz said, doubling over with laughter. "You go, girl!"

Hearing the noise behind him, Mr Tyler stopped and turned round. He saw Willow, who ran up to him and jumped up.

"No – Willow!" Liz shouted, her laughter suddenly gone.

"I'll get her," said Neil.

He started to run. Neil couldn't help remembering the fuss Mr Tyler had made about Jake, and how he had accused the lively young dog of being dangerous.

Now he was batting irritably at Willow, who kept on jumping up as if she too thought he wanted to play with her. He thrust a foot out, not exactly kicking Willow, but trying to push

her away. Yapping excitedly, Willow dropped the envelope and grabbed the bottom of his trouser leg. She began tugging at it with high-pitched little growly noises.

Before Neil could reach her, Mr Tyler shook his leg vigorously until Willow fell off. Then he aimed a kick at her – a real, hard kick this time. His boot caught Willow in the side and she rolled over on the turf, whimpering loudly.

Neil flung himself down on his knees beside her. "If you've hurt her, I'll report you to the police!" he shouted.

To his surprise, Mr Tyler was grinning. "*You'll* report *me* to the police? That's a good one. I'll be the one doing the reporting."

Liz came up and squatted down beside Willow, resting a hand soothingly on her head. "You just dare!" she said.

"Dare?" said Mr Tyler. "Why shouldn't I? Your dog just attacked me, young woman, in front of a witness." The other man nodded. Mr Tyler went on triumphantly, "That means I can get the police to move you off this land. If I were you, I'd start packing up right now!"

Chapter Six

Willow was still lying on the grass. Liz and Neil bent over her and touched the dog's side where Mr Tyler had kicked her. Willow whimpered. Emily and Toby gathered round anxiously.

"She's hurt!" cried Liz.

Neil glanced briefly after the transport engineer, who was storming off down the hill, and then turned his attention back to the little dog. He patted her side gently and she licked his hand.

"I can't feel anything broken," he said, "but I reckon Mike Turner had better take a look at her."

"He's your local vet, right?" said Liz, pulling a

mobile phone out of her jacket pocket. "How can I get in touch with him?"

"His surgery's in Compton," said Neil, "but he's doing a routine inspection at King Street this morning." He glanced at his watch. "We should just be able to catch him."

Liz gave him her mobile phone, and Neil punched in the King Street Kennels' number. Bob Parker answered almost immediately.

"Hi, Dad. Is Mike still there?"

"Just finishing off now," said Bob. "What's the problem?"

Neil explained what had happened.

"I'll tell Mike," Bob said when he had finished. "He'll come up right away. Keep the dog calm until he gets there."

Neil passed the message on to Liz.

"Thank goodness!" she said. "I don't know what I'd do if anything happened to Willow."

She went back to her tent and fetched Willow a bowl of water. Willow lapped it gratefully and seemed to be feeling more comfortable.

It wasn't long before Neil could see two figures climbing the hill from the exercise field. He nudged Emily. "Look who's here."

Kate was with Mike Turner. Seeing her point towards the camp, Neil guessed that she had come to show him just where he would find Willow.

As they drew closer, Glen hurried over to meet her and they stayed talking together while Mike Turner came to look at his patient.

Willow was more relaxed by now and she raised her head as Mike knelt beside her. Her eyes were bright with interest.

"Neil, you said she was kicked?" Mike began. "She doesn't look to be in too much pain." He let Willow sniff his fingers, and then stroked her head. "Hi, there, girl. Let's have a look at you, shall we?"

Liz showed Mike where the kick had landed, and Mike felt Willow's ribs and stomach gently. Willow whimpered again softly, but didn't try to pull away. Neil stroked her head to calm her while Liz watched anxiously.

"I wondered if she might have broken a rib," Mike said at last, "but there's no swelling and I can't feel any movement from a broken bone. All the same, I'd like her to come to the surgery for an X-ray."

"Right," said Liz. "I'll come with you. Or—" She hesitated, and looked even more worried. "I'm in charge here, and we might be having a visit from the police. I really shouldn't leave."

59

"No problem," said Mike. "I'll take her and you can come in to collect her when it's convenient. Give me your mobile number – I'll ring you if she needs treatment."

Liz pulled out a scrap of paper and a pen from her jacket pocket and wrote down the number.

"I feel terrible about this," she said. "Willow wouldn't have been hurt if it wasn't for this protest and now I can't come and look after her properly." She gave Neil an apologetic look. "Maybe you were right that I shouldn't be keeping a dog up here."

"It's not your fault Willow's been injured," said Neil.

"No, it's that horrible Mr Tyler!" said Emily.

Liz shrugged. "Even so . . ."

She was looking so downhearted that Neil said, "Would it help if I went with Willow? She knows me – we get on fine, don't we, Willow? Then I could bring her back later, if she's OK."

"Would you really, Neil?" Liz gave Neil a brilliant smile. "That would be a big help."

"All part of the Puppy Patrol service," said Neil, grinning.

Liz looked puzzled. "Puppy Patrol?"

"That's what everybody calls the Parkers,"

Mike explained. "Wherever there are dogs in need in Compton, you'll find the Puppy Patrol!"

Mike Turner drove Neil and Willow back to King Street Kennels when the examination was over. The X-ray had not shown any broken bones and by the time she trotted into the kitchen with Neil, Willow was her usual lively self.

Emily jumped up from the kitchen table where her project was spread out and crouched down to rumple Willow's ears. Jake leapt out of his basket and scampered round the kitchen, barking as if he expected a game.

"She's OK, then?" Emily said, giving Willow a hug and giggling as the little dog licked her face.

"She's fine. I thought you were staying up at the camp to do your project?"

"Toby had to go home, so I came back to write up my notes." She held up a sheet of paper covered with her neat handwriting and little sketches of flowers.

"Did the police come?" Neil asked.

Emily shook her head. "Not while I was there. Maybe that awful Mr Tyler didn't dare report Willow after all."

"Maybe." Neil wasn't so sure.

Just then Bob came into the kitchen. With

the back door open, Neil could hear a spate of furious yapping coming from the kennel blocks.

"Let me guess!" he said. "Sugar and Spice!"

Bob made a face. "They've been at it all morning. It's enough to give anybody a headache. Still," he added, grinning, "Mrs Jepson gets back from her long weekend tomorrow, so we'll be saying goodbye to the little darlings."

Thinking about Sugar and Spice made Neil remember Mr Jepson's odd behaviour. "I'm sure Mr Jepson knows more about this new road than he's letting on," he said. "He really doesn't want anybody to find out why he voted for the ridgeway route."

Emily's eyes widened. "Why not?"

"Well . . ." Bob scratched his beard thoughtfully. "Maybe he owns property along the ridgeway, and he could sell it to the council at a good profit. Or maybe he owns land along the other route, and doesn't want to sell it. But—"

"But wouldn't that be wrong?" Emily asked. "Are councillors allowed to do that?"

"You're right," said her dad. "It would be wrong. It might even be criminal."

"Hey!" said Neil. "You mean Mr Jepson could go to prison?"

"Now come on, let's not get excited," said Bob. "I know Mr Jepson can be a real pain in the neck, but I'm sure he wouldn't go that far."

"No?" said Emily disbelievingly.

"No," Bob insisted. "He wouldn't. And *please* don't go round discussing this with anyone else. You could get into serious trouble."

"OK, Dad, keep your beard on," Neil said. "We won't. But whatever he's doing," he added determinedly, "we've got to put a stop to it."

When lunch was over, Neil and Emily took Willow back to the camp. Neil had already phoned Liz to say that the little dog was all right, but Liz still ran her hands anxiously over Willow's side as if she couldn't believe it. Willow jumped up to cover her face with enthusiastic licks.

"Hey, girl, take it easy!" said Liz, laughing. To Neil, she added, "I'm really grateful that you went with her. It took a load off my mind."

"No problem!" said Neil. "We got on fine, didn't we, Willow?"

Willow barked in agreement.

Another bark answered her – not from Jake,

who was sitting quietly by Neil's side, but from a different dog, some way off.

Neil turned round. "I know that dog!"

He was right. Coming up the path towards the camp were Sergeant Moorhead of Compton police force and his police dog Sherlock.

Sergeant Moorhead was in charge of the Compton police dog squad. Nobody who saw him with Sherlock could doubt that he loved dogs, and he had often helped the Parkers with doggy problems. All the same, Neil was not pleased to see him now.

"What does *he* want?" Neil said.

Liz gave Willow a last pat and straightened up. "Mr Tyler must have reported us after all."

A few of the other protesters began to gather round as they realized the camp was to have a visit from the police. Glen was among them, and he had Kate with him.

Emily gave Neil a poke. "Kate's still here," she said with a grin. "Do you think it's all right?"

"Dunno," whispered Neil. He had other things on his mind as he watched Sergeant Moorhead approach. He wanted to know what Mr Tyler had said about Willow; he was pretty sure it would all be lies.

Sergeant Moorhead halted as he reached the group who were waiting for him. Sherlock sat obediently beside him, and Neil went over to offer him a dog treat. As Sherlock crunched it up, Neil ran his hands over the dog's shiny black-and-tan coat, admiring the intelligence in his amber eyes. He couldn't believe that Sergeant Moorhead would do anything bad to Willow when he had such a brilliant dog of his own to work with.

"Which of you is Ms Hart?" the sergeant asked.

"I am," said Liz. "Is there a problem, Sergeant?"

"I've had a report that you're keeping a dangerous dog up here," Sergeant Moorhead said.

"*Dangerous*?" Neil looked up from Sherlock. "Willow's not dangerous!"

"Willow?" The sergeant was gazing around, as if he expected to see something huge, like a Rottweiler or a Doberman, come leaping out of the trees.

"This is Willow," said Liz.

Sergeant Moorhead looked down. Willow was sitting at his feet, looking back at him with bright eyes and tongue lolling out.

"This is the . . . er . . . dangerous dog?" he asked.

"She's the only dog we've got," said Liz.

Neil thought Sergeant Moorhead was going to burst out laughing, but he straightened his face and bent over, holding out his hand for Willow to sniff. For a moment he ruffled her wiry, white curls, and then he faced Liz again.

"Ms Hart, I've had a complaint that your dog attacked an employee of the local council."

"Mr Tyler, the chief transport engineer," Liz said calmly.

"You admit that your dog attacked him?"

"I admit that my dog tried to have a game with him. She grabbed his trouser leg – after he stuck his foot out at her. She thought he wanted to play. And then he kicked her, so hard that she had to be X-rayed by the vet to make sure that her ribs weren't broken. Did Mr Tyler tell you that, Sergeant?"

"No, he didn't." Sergeant Moorhead looked thoughtfully down at Willow.

"You can ask Mike Turner," Neil put in. "Mr Tyler just doesn't know how to handle dogs, that's all."

The sergeant nodded. "I don't doubt your word, Ms Hart," he said, "or that you believe your version of events. But—"

"My version of events?" Liz interrupted indignantly. She gestured towards the group of protesters standing nearby. "I've got plenty of witnesses."

"Sure she has," said Glen. "Ask any of us."

"I know," said Sergeant Moorhead. "But Mr Tyler has a witness too. And none of you are exactly unbiased, are you? I have to think what would happen if this case came to court. Mr Tyler reported that your dog attacked him, and it does seem that there was an incident. He isn't just making it up. How serious the incident was, or how badly your dog was provoked, would be matters for the court to decide."

"But can't you see, Sergeant?" Liz was getting even angrier. "Mr Tyler is just using this. He wants an excuse to get rid of us!"

"Ms Hart," said Sergeant Moorhead, "he was talking in terms of having the dog destroyed."

"That's awful!" Emily cried. She knelt beside Willow and flung her arms round the little dog.

"It's that serious?" Liz asked.

"No," said Sergeant Moorhead. "Now that I've seen the dog, I'm fairly sure it's not that serious. There's no question of destroying Willow. But the fact remains that an attack was made on an employee of the local authority who are the owners of the land. You could be charged with breach of the peace."

"What's that?" Neil asked.

"It means that Ms Hart and her friends have been causing an unreasonable disturbance," Sergeant Moorhead explained.

Liz snorted. "And if the road's built? That won't be a breach of the peace?"

"Not according to the law." Sergeant Moorhead took a deep breath and looked round the group of protesters. "I'm afraid I have to ask you to be out of here by tomorrow."

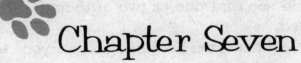

Chapter Seven

"**D**oes that mean you'll have to give up, Liz?" Neil asked. "You'll have to let them build the road through here?"

Everyone was watching Sergeant Moorhead as he and Sherlock retreated down the hill. Neil guessed that the police officer hadn't enjoyed the interview, but he didn't have much choice. His job was to uphold the law.

"No, it doesn't," said Liz. "I expected some sort of attempt to get rid of us. But we haven't done anything wrong, and we're not going." She swung round to face her supporters. "We stick it out! Right?" she called out.

Most people shouted back, "Right!" though

Neil could see that one or two of them looked undecided.

Liz waved her arms beckoning to everyone to gather round her, and hopped up on to an upturned box that someone had been using as a seat.

"Listen, everybody. It's getting tough, but we knew it would get tough. We're not giving in!"

A woman at the back of the crowd objected, "I've got children to look after."

"Right," Liz replied. "And that's important. So anybody with responsibilities, or with any doubts at all, go now. No hard feelings. Do what you can to protest in other ways. But those of us who can, we're staying! We don't want this road, and we're going to let the council know that. If they want us out of here, they'll have to carry us out!"

The woman who had spoken, and one or two other people, split off from the group around Liz and started to pack up their things, but most of the protesters stayed where they were.

Glen let out a cheer. "We're with you, Liz!"

Neil saw that Kate was standing just behind him, with her hands thrust into her pockets and a moody expression on her face.

"Right!" said Liz. "The first thing we've got to do is make sure that people know what's happening. I think we should write a press release and send it to all the local TV and radio stations." She jumped down off the box. "Let's get to it."

She dived into her tent; Glen was starting to follow her when Neil saw Kate tug him by the sleeve. He heard Glen say, "Yes? What's the matter?"

"Can't you see what's the matter?" Kate sounded really upset. "Glen Paget, do you really have to ask?"

Glen looked bewildered, "Honestly, Kate—"

"You've been stuck up this hill for nearly a week. I've hardly seen you. And now you're staying here when it looks as if you'll be arrested!"

"But it's important, Kate. I can't let Liz down when she's relying on me."

"Let Liz down!" Kate was nearly crying. "What about letting me down?"

Neil and Emily gave each other a worried look. The last thing they'd expected was for Glen and Kate to start quarrelling.

Glen sounded as if he still didn't understand what was upsetting Kate so much. "I thought you would agree with what we're doing," he said. "You don't want a road here, do you?"

"No, of course I don't, but—"

"Then you can see that I have to do something about it." He tried to take Kate's hand. "Kate, why don't you stay? We could—"

Kate snatched her hand away. "I can't stay when I have a job to do. And a wedding to get ready for – if there's going to be a wedding at all!"

Glen looked stunned. "Kate!"

"Well?" Kate's tears had overflowed, and she scrubbed at her face with the back of her hand. "We can't get married, can we, if you're in prison?"

"But I'm not going to be."

"You don't know that! You heard Sergeant Moorhead! Or maybe it's all an excuse and you're staying up here because you'd rather be with Liz?"

Glen stood gaping at her. "Kate, that is absolutely not true!"

"I don't believe you!" Kate was sobbing now. She tugged her engagement ring off and thrust it at Glen. He didn't take it, and it fell on the grass. "I'm going – and I don't want to see you again. Ever!"

Still sobbing, she turned and ran down the path.

Glen took a step after her. "Kate! Kate, come back!"

Kate took no notice. Glen stooped, picked up the ring, and then stood turning it round and round in his fingers. Neil thought he looked just as upset as Kate, but after a minute he put the ring in his pocket and went to look for Liz.

Neil wanted to be around when the Jepsons came to collect Sugar and Spice, so the next day he helped his mother to give the little Westies a brush before they went home. It was hard to get the tangles out of Spice's coat when he kept trying to leap off the grooming table or turn his head to bite the brush.

"They're still far too fat," said Carole, as she ran the comb through the curls on the top of Sugar's head and tied them up with a pink bow.

Neil thought bows on dogs were disgusting, but Mrs Jepson would have made a fuss if her little darlings weren't properly prettified.

"They'd be worse if they didn't get the right food when they come here," he said.

"Or at Pretty Paws," said Carole fairly. "At least Mrs Sparrow feeds them a sensible diet now, even if she does put perfume in the bath water."

Just then a tap came on the treatment room door and Jane Hammond opened it. Neil and Carole grabbed at the two Westies as they both made a sudden leap for freedom.

"Sorry," said Jane. "I didn't realize you had those two in here." She flourished a folder of papers. "I brought these round. We've been organizing a petition and I knew you would want to sign it. Maybe you'd like to keep some sheets in the office for your clients?"

"Of course," said Carole. "Have you given some to Mike Turner?"

"And some to school?" Neil added.

Jane smiled. "Yes, they're all over Compton. And when we're ready, we're going to march to the town hall to present all the signatures."

"Hundreds of sheets, in sacks!" Neil said, laughing. "Dumped on Mr Tyler's doorstep. That'd be ace!"

Jane left the petition sheets and said goodbye. Not much later the door of the treatment room opened again and Bob poked his head round it.

"Are the cute little doggie-woggies ready? The Jepsons are here."

74

Neil clipped on Spice's lead, while his mum did the same with Sugar. "Ready as they'll ever be," he said.

As he led Spice across the courtyard, Neil wondered for the thousandth time how he could find out what Mr Jepson gained from having the road built across the ridgeway. Mr Jepson certainly wouldn't tell him directly!

The Jepsons were standing outside the door to the office. Mrs Jepson, dressed in a bright turquoise tracksuit, held her arms out when she saw her dogs trotting towards her.

"How are Mummy's little cutesie-wutesies? Come to Mummy, my pets!"

She scooped up Spice and planted a sloppy kiss on the end of his nose, while Carole handed Sugar's lead to Mr Jepson.

Carole said, "I hope you're feeling better, Mrs Jepson."

"Oh, yes, so much better! Dr Upton at Happydale is such a wonderful man! He has a gift for relieving you of stress – I always come out of Happydale feeling like a new woman! You should try it, Mrs Parker, really you should."

"I'll think about it," said Carole drily.

"Of course all Dr Upton's patients were very worried when we thought Happydale would have to close down," Mrs Jepson burbled on, trying to grab the paw that Spice was sticking in her ear. "But now that horrid road is going somewhere else, everything will be all right."

Neil stiffened. He saw his mum and dad glance at each other.

"What's that about the road?" Bob asked.

"Oh, hadn't you heard? There was a plan to build a road that would have gone right through the grounds at Happydale – practically past poor Dr Upton's front door! But Norman's on the council, of course, and he soon put a stop to that, didn't you, Norman?"

She gave Mr Jepson a sickly smile. Neil felt himself beginning to grin as he looked at Mr Jepson. He was standing frozen, with a face like a frog.

Neil realized that Mrs Jepson had just told him what he wanted to know. The other route for the bypass, that would leave the ridgeway untouched, would have cut across her beloved health farm. Now he understood why Mr Jepson had voted against it.

Mr Jepson coughed. "Yes, well, we'd better be getting on."

He took the Westies' vaccination certificates, which Bob handed to him, and followed Mrs

Jepson to their car.

Neil fell into step beside him. "Wasn't it lucky that you were able to save the health farm?" he said chattily.

Mr Jepson grunted.

"I bet Jake Fielding would like to write that up for the *Compton News*," Neil suggested. "To talk to all the people who go there."

Mr Jepson's face was slowly turning a dusky red. "If I see anything about this in the *Compton News*—"

"You wouldn't say that if you weren't ashamed of the way you voted," said Neil. "You were just thinking about the health farm, and not about the ridgeway, and the wildlife, and all the fun that people have up there."

Mr Jepson halted in the driveway and prodded Neil in the chest. "Now you listen to me—"

"Norman!" Mrs Jepson trilled. She was already in the car. "Are you coming, Norman?"

Mr Jepson backed away from Neil, towards the car. "How I vote is my business. You keep your nose out of it! And stay away from that reporter."

He shoved Sugar roughly into the back of the car, got into the driver's seat and slammed the door. Neil could see that he was giving Mrs Jepson a piece of his mind as they drove away.

Neil stood looking down the drive after the car had disappeared. He couldn't help grinning. Emily would kick herself for missing the look on Mr Jepson's face.

Maybe now Mr Jepson would change the way he voted next time the issue came up. And that might mean the ridgeway would survive. Neil heaved a huge sigh of relief.

But he knew that didn't solve the immediate problem. While the protesters stayed in the camp, Glen would stay with them. Kate would still be angry with him. Unless something happened quickly, Neil knew, there wasn't going to be a wedding.

On Wednesday morning, Jake woke Neil by planting his front paws on his chest and swiping his tongue over Neil's face while he still lay in bed.

"Gerr-off," Neil muttered, gently shoving Jake to one side as he crawled out of bed. He knew he had to get up early to walk Jake before school started on the first day of the new term, but that didn't mean he had to like it.

Reluctantly, he pulled his Meadowbank

78

School sweatshirt over his head and began groping for his trainers.

In the kitchen, he found that Kate had already arrived for work and was making herself a cup of coffee. She looked tired.

"Hi, Neil," she said, managing a smile. "School this morning?"

"Yeah, worse luck." Neil felt embarrassed talking to Kate, knowing she had split up with Glen but not knowing what to say about it. "I thought I'd give Jake a run on the ridgeway first, though."

That obviously hadn't been the right thing to say. Kate's mouth tightened, and she sat at the table to drink her coffee without another word.

Neil fed Jake and poured a glass of milk to keep himself going until breakfast. Soon Emily appeared, and fetched herself a glass while she checked her school bag.

"Are you taking Jake out?" she asked.

Neil nodded. "I thought I'd go up to the ridgeway," he said. "Just to see if the camp's still there."

Emily finished her drink. "I'll come with you. Kate, why don't you come as well?"

Kate looked up at her, hesitated, and shook her head. "There's loads to do here."

"Come on," said Neil. "You want to know what's happening, don't you?"

"Yes, but . . ."

"It's one of your favourite places," Emily said.

"It was," said Kate sadly. She finished her coffee and stood up. "Well – all right. Just for a quick run with Jake."

The morning was misty, but as they crossed the exercise field, the sun began to break through. Halfway up the ridge, Neil halted, panting, and watched Jake rooting around in the hollows for imaginary rabbits. All the leaves were out on the trees, and birds were singing. Everything was peaceful. Neil couldn't understand why anyone would want to destroy this magical place.

"What are we going to do about Mr Jepson and the health farm?" Emily asked as they started to climb again. Neil had told her what he had discovered the day before. "We can't just assume he'll change his vote. Think of the grief he'd get from Mrs Jepson!"

"Think of the grief he'd get if the whole story was in the *Compton News*," said Neil. "He'd probably have to resign from the council."

"Yes, but—" Emily broke off as they reached the top of the hill and saw the tents of the protest camp still pitched along the edge of the wood. "You see!" she said. "Sergeant Moorhead hasn't arrested them after all."

"Yet," said Neil. He couldn't imagine that Sergeant Moorhead would make a threat and not carry it out, however much he sympathized with the protesters. The deadline for the camp to break up had passed; Neil was sure that something would happen soon.

He wasn't prepared for how soon it would be.

As he and Emily walked towards the camp, with Kate a few paces behind, he heard a dog barking, and saw Sergeant Moorhead with Sherlock appearing from the opposite direction. Behind him was a group of other uniformed policemen. Neil recognized Constable Grey and Constable Edwards.

"No!" Emily grabbed Neil's arm. "They can't!"

She let Neil go again and dashed towards the camp, shouting, "Liz! Liz!"

Jake bounded after her, barking furiously. More barking answered him and Willow shot out of Liz's tent.

Neil ran after his sister. As he arrived beside Liz's tent the flap was pushed back and Liz crawled out. She was blinking and her long dark hair was all over the place.

"What—" she began. "What's happening? Willow, be quiet."

Willow, dancing around in wild excitement, took no notice. Liz scrambled to her feet and saw Sergeant Moorhead approaching with his squad of police. Other people were crawling out of their tents, trying to work out what was happening.

"Liz, do something!" said Emily.

Liz tossed her long hair back. "Make for the trees!" she shouted.

The protesters were still too bewildered to obey her right away. While they hesitated, Sergeant Moorhead broke into a run. "Head them off!" he yelled.

Some of the protesters dashed for the platforms, but Sergeant Moorhead's men managed to get between them and the edge of the wood. Neil saw Glen trying to dive through a gap between the policemen; Constable Edwards grabbed him, spun him round, and started to march him off down the slope.

Neil couldn't help looking round for Kate. She was some way away, watching from under the trees. She looked as if she didn't want to be involved, but couldn't bear to leave and not see what happened.

The dash for the trees had failed. As the protesters realized that the police were guarding the platforms, some of them started to run away, and the police let them go. Others made their way across to Liz, who was standing with her arms folded, confronting Sergeant Moorhead. Neil went to stand beside her.

"I'm sorry, Ms Hart," the sergeant said. "I gave you a time limit to be out of here and you ignored it. You haven't left me with much choice." He hesitated and added, "If you leave now, there won't be any more trouble."

Liz stood her ground. "No."

"Then you and your friends will have to come with me to the police station."

"OK." Liz had a determined look on her face. She looked round at the remains of the group. "No violence, remember?" she said. "But we don't leave unless they make us."

Reluctantly, as if it was the last thing he wanted to do, Sergeant Moorhead put a hand on her shoulder.

Neil said, "Sergeant Moorhead, you can't do this! You know it's wrong."

"It's the law, Neil," Sergeant Moorhead said firmly.

Neil clenched his fists. He was furious. The protesters weren't doing any harm. All they wanted was to keep the countryside for everyone to enjoy. Because Mr Tyler had lied about Willow, the police were breaking everything up, and there was nothing he could do to stop them.

As the police closed in on Liz, Willow started barking again. Jake joined in, and Emily grabbed his collar. Neil tried to catch hold of Willow, but she shied away from him.

"Catch that dog!" Sergeant Moorhead shouted. "Bring it along!"

Liz looked round wildly as two policemen dragged her away. "Neil!" she shouted. "Get Willow! Don't let them take Willow!"

The little white dog was dancing around Constable Grey's feet, avoiding his hands as he tried to grab her. Neil swooped down and picked her up in his arms. "Don't worry, Liz!" he called. "I'll look after her!"

"Give me that dog!" Constable Grey ordered.

Neil ignored him and ducked under his outstretched arms. He hurtled towards the trees, and nearly cannoned into Kate, who was still standing on the edge of the commotion, looking bewildered.

"Willow!" Neil gasped. "We've got to save Willow."

Kate followed him as he headed for the tree with Willow's platform.

"Trees, girl!" he said, putting Willow down. "Up you go!" He glanced back to where Constable Grey was blundering through the undergrowth towards them. "Quick!"

"Here, let me go first," said Kate.

She put one foot in the fork of the trunk, clambered up the sloping branch and hauled herself over the edge of the platform. From there she held out a hand to Willow. "Here, Willow! Come on, girl!"

Willow suddenly decided to play the game, and scrambled upwards until Kate could grab her. Neil followed, managing to avoid Constable Grey as the policeman grabbed at his foot.

"Come down!" Constable Grey gasped. "That dog's dangerous."

Neil paused halfway up the sloping branch. "No, she's not."

"You do as you're told, young man, or—" Constable Grey broke off as a shout came from the camp. He gave Neil a last angry look and headed back through the trees. Neil watched him go, and then pulled himself the rest of the way up the tree.

On the platform, he found Kate sitting with her back against a branch, and Willow in her arms. "Quiet now," she said, patting the little dog soothingly. "Neil, have you got a titbit?"

Neil pulled out a handful of dog treats and gave them to Kate. Crouching on the edge of the platform, he peered through the leaves.

He couldn't see anything but the back of the nearest tent, but he could hear shouting and trampling feet. Gradually the sound died away, until there was silence. Then Neil heard Emily's voice calling his name. She sounded upset.

"Over here!" he yelled. "In Willow's tree!"

Emily came to stand at the bottom of the tree. Jake trotted after her, and put his paws up on the trunk.

"They've gone now," Emily said. She pulled out a handkerchief and scrubbed at her eyes. "All except Constable Grey. When you come down, he'll take Willow away."

Neil glanced at Kate. Whether there was a police guard on the camp or not, he didn't want to come down and pretend it didn't matter if the developers wrecked the ridgeway.

"I'm not coming down," he said. "I'm staying up here until they change the plans for the new road."

Chapter Eight

"**Y**ou don't *have* to do this, you know," said Neil.

Kate was still leaning back against the branch, her arms wrapped round her knees. "Oh, yes, I do," she said. "I don't want the road here any more than you do."

Emily had taken Jake and gone to tell their mum and dad what had happened. School would be starting in about twenty minutes. Neil wondered how much trouble he would be in for bunking off.

Willow had settled down happily on the platform and was snoozing with her nose on her paws. Neil rested one hand on her rough coat and tried to decide what to do next.

He had no idea how long it would take for the council to make the final decision about the road. "This could take weeks," he muttered.

Kate shrugged. "So it takes weeks."

She didn't seem to be asking herself what they would do about food, or whether they could sleep on the platform. Neil tried hard to make himself ignore those questions, even though he was already starving after missing breakfast. Whatever it took, he was staying put.

He could just make out the figure of Constable Grey, standing guard at the edge of the wood, and before very long the young police officer turned and made his way towards the tree. He was tall, with wiry black hair, and just now he looked fed up.

"Come on, lad, let's be having you," he said. "You're not doing any good up there, you know. Come down now and we'll say no more about it."

"And what about Willow?" Neil asked suspiciously.

"There's been a complaint against her," Constable Grey said. "She'll have to be kept under control."

"She is under control." Neil put his arms

round Willow protectively. "You're not taking her away."

"There's still a case to answer," Constable Grey said stubbornly.

He stood staring up at Neil for a minute longer, frustration written all over him. Then he swung round abruptly and stamped off, back to the abandoned camp.

When he had gone, everything was very quiet. The breeze rustled the branches of the trees and birds were singing. Then, from a distance, Neil heard a dog barking, followed by the sound of footsteps coming through the trees. His mother's voice called, "Neil!"

"Over here!" he shouted.

Carole Parker appeared with Bev, and four of the boarding dogs on leads. She strode across to the foot of the tree and stood looking up at Neil with an exasperated expression on her face.

"Neil Parker, have you completely taken leave of your senses?"

"Sorry, Mum," Neil said.

"Never mind 'sorry'! I want you down from there right now."

Neil moved back from the edge of the platform. "No." He met his mother's angry stare and added, "I've got to do this. It's for the ridgeway."

Carole let out a long sigh. "Kate, can't you talk some sense into him?"

Kate reddened. "I'm really sorry, Carole, but I can't. I'm staying as well."

Carole took a deep breath, seemed not to know what to say, and turned helplessly to Bev. "What am I going to do?"

Bev looked serious, but Neil hadn't missed the twinkle in her eyes, and he guessed she was on his side. "There isn't much you can do, Carole. They'll come down when they're hungry."

Neil wanted to say, *I'm hungry now!* but he resisted.

"Right," Carole said determinedly. "Let's see how long it takes. On the other hand, Neil, I'd better take Willow home with me."

"No!" said Neil. "Sergeant Moorhead wants to take her to the police station."

Carole gave it some thought. Then she gave the boarding dogs' leads to Bev, and disappeared in the direction of Liz's tent.

A moment later she was back, with Willow's dog food, bowls and bottles of water. "I don't see why the dog should suffer just because you're being stupid," she said.

"Thanks, Mum." Neil climbed down just far enough to take the food from her and retreated to the platform, where Willow sat up, bright-eyed at the thought of being fed. "Er . . . Liz hasn't left any of her food there, has she?"

"I wouldn't be surprised," Carole said, as she unfastened the boarding dogs' leads again. She set off through the woods, and called back over her shoulder, "If you want it, Neil, you'll have to come down and get it yourself!"

Bev started to follow her, and then turned back with a finger to her lips. She took a bar of chocolate out of her jacket pocket and tossed it up to Neil.

Neil caught it and mouthed, "Thanks!"

Bev grinned at him and followed his mother.

It was nearly midday when Neil heard more footsteps approaching. This time Bob appeared through the trees and came to stand underneath the platform.

Neil looked down at him. "I'm sorry, Dad, but I'm not coming down."

"Did I ask you to? I thought you might like to know what's going on, that's all."

Neil glanced quickly at Kate. "Sure we would," he said.

"Well," said Bob, "I phoned the school to let Mr Hamley know where you are."

Neil winced, imagining how his head teacher would react to that.

"After that," Bob went on, "I spent most of the morning trying to get hold of Sergeant Moorhead. I wanted to know what was happening to Glen and the other protesters, and whether the two of you are committing an offence. But he was too busy to come to the phone until just now."

"What did he say?" Kate asked.

"The people he arrested this morning will be released for now, but in the long term they could face prison or a fine, because they didn't leave when they were told to."

"Prison!" Kate exclaimed, looking horrified.

"Just for sticking up for what you believe in?" said Neil.

"That's the law, Neil," Bob said. "Whether it will come to that, I don't know. As far as you're concerned, nothing's clear, because you weren't among the people who were originally told to leave."

"And what about Willow?" Neil said. "Did you ask about her?"

"No," said Bob. "Sergeant Moorhead didn't

mention her, so neither did I. But I had a word with Constable Grey just now. He's guarding the camp to make sure the protesters don't come back, and he thinks Mr Tyler's determined to bring the case to court."

Neil wasn't surprised to hear that.

"You know, your mother's very worried about you," said Bob.

"We're fine, aren't we, Kate? Hungry, that's all."

"Well . . ." Neil noticed for the first time that his father had a backpack over one shoulder; he unslung it and passed it up to Neil. "Your mum said you were stubborn enough to stick it out without any food, so she told me to bring you this."

"Hey, Dad, thanks!"

Neil fell on the backpack and pulled out a box of sandwiches, some apples, chocolate biscuits and a bottle of orange squash.

Bob grinned at him. "Well, I've got work to do. We can't all lounge around up trees. I expect Emily will bring Jake to see you when school's over."

Neil grinned back at him. He suddenly felt better about everything. "Great, Dad. Tell Mum we're OK, won't you?"

Bob raised a hand and strode off. Neil opened up the box of sandwiches and held it out to Kate. "Ham or cheese and chutney?"

The afternoon wore on. Neil started to realize that one of his biggest problems would be sitting here for hours on end with nothing to do. He even started feeling sorry that he hadn't gone to school to see his friends.

Willow was getting restless, too. Neil was beginning to wonder if he dared sneak down to give her some exercise when he heard voices and saw Emily with his Border collie Jake and Jake Fielding the reporter. Behind them were Chris Wilson and Hasheem Lindon, two of his friends from Meadowbank School.

"Hi, Neil, Kate," said Jake Fielding. He dug into a pocket of his baggy denim jacket for a spare lens. "This is going to make a great picture!"

"I told Jake all about what happened this morning," Emily said.

"And I've spoken to the police." Jake Fielding was grinning. "There hasn't been so much going on around here for years!"

"Trust Neil!" said Chris. "Are you OK up there, mate?"

"Fine, thanks," said Neil.

"Hey, Neil," said Hasheem. "Remember Mrs Sharpe telling us about how we're all descended from monkeys? I didn't believe it, but I do now!"

"Oh, very funny," said Neil with a sigh.

Jake the dog was barking and scrabbling at the tree, as if he wanted to climb up to Neil, but he wasn't as good at climbing as Willow. Neil couldn't even reach down to pat him.

"Sorry, boy," he said. "Emily will look after you for now."

He couldn't help wondering what would happen to Jake's training programme if he wasn't there to oversee it.

Emily passed some more food up to Neil and Kate while Jake Fielding checked the settings on his light meter and fiddled with the exposure on his camera.

"Are you really going to stay here until the council change their minds?" he asked.

"Not if he knows what's good for him," a new voice said.

Neil looked up to see Mr Hamley, his head teacher. He was wearing his country squire outfit of a waxed jacket and tweed cap. His Dalmatian, Dotty, was dancing around his feet, and when she saw her friends around the tree she let off a series of excited barks.

Neil smiled weakly. "Hello, Mr Hamley."

Mr Hamley walked forward and planted himself at the foot of Neil's tree. "Neil, I don't know what you think you're doing, but you can't stay here like this and miss school. Come down from there right now."

Neil felt awful. At Meadowbank, you did what Mr Hamley told you – and fast if you had any sense. He swallowed. "No, sir. I've got to stay here. I'm not going to let them build the road."

Jake Fielding clicked his camera. "Mr Hamley, could you move this way a bit? Then I'll get one of you as well."

"No I couldn't!" Mr Hamley stepped back rapidly. "I'm not having the school involved in this. I suppose, Neil, that you had to make your protest in a Meadowbank uniform?"

Neil swallowed again. "I didn't plan it, sir."

Mr Hamley snorted. "I suppose you know that your parents are legally obliged to send you to school? If you stick to this silly behaviour for very much longer, they're going to be in trouble." He paused, but Neil had nothing to say. "Give it some thought," he added. "And make sure I see you back in school tomorrow."

He turned to go, but his dignified exit was

spoilt by Dotty, who had managed to scramble up the tree as far as the fork in the trunk, and was stuck there, whining. Red-faced, Mr Hamley hauled her down, clipped on her lead and strode off.

Jake Fielding was grinning broadly and scribbling in his notebook. Neil shuddered to think what might be in the next issue of the *Compton News.*

All the same, he thought, *I'm not coming down. Not for Mr Hamley or anybody else.*

It was starting to get dark. Neil was wondering how they'd keep warm for the night, when he heard more movement in the undergrowth and Bob Parker appeared, with Glen just behind him.

"Glen!" Kate exclaimed. "Are you all right? What happened?"

Just for a minute, Neil could see, she had forgotten about the quarrel. Then she looked annoyed with herself, and wouldn't look at Glen when he came to stand under the platform.

"Sergeant Moorhead won't press charges," he said. "He let us go – all except Liz. She's still answering questions, because she was the organizer." He hesitated, and sounded embarrassed as he added, "Kate, won't you come down?"

Kate shook her head.

"We need to talk this through," Glen said. "Somewhere private. Please?"

"No," said Kate.

Glen gave Bob a helpless look.

Bob beckoned to Neil to come to one end of the platform and said, "Glen and I came up to sort out the stuff that the protesters left. You two can borrow sleeping bags if you're determined to stay, and I'm going to sleep here as well. Your mum says she wants somebody with sense to keep an eye on you."

While he was talking, Glen had moved closer to Kate, and was saying something in a low voice. It was the best they could do for a private conversation. Kate was still hardly speaking, and Glen was looking more and more harassed.

Finally he said, loud enough for Neil and Bob to hear, "If our case had gone to court, we could have been in prison for three months, or fined over two thousand pounds. Is that what you want to happen to you?"

"You should have thought of that before you decided to spend a whole week here!" said Kate.

"Look, Kate—" Glen broke off. "I don't know what to say. I'll come up and see you again tomorrow."

He turned and walked off, his shoulders sagging. Kate didn't say goodbye, even when Willow let out a sharp bark. She sat with her back to Neil, and Neil thought she was crying. He didn't try to talk to her while Bob went to fetch sleeping bags from the abandoned tents. He didn't know what to say.

He was at a loss as to how anybody could put things right.

Chapter Nine

Moonlight shone through the leaves. Neil lay in his sleeping bag, but he was finding it impossible to sleep up the tree. Too many thoughts were churning through his mind. Would they really be able to stop the road? Would Kate and Glen get together again? Would Mr Tyler make the court believe that Willow was dangerous?

The platform was hard. For the thousandth time Neil tried to wriggle into a more comfortable position, and felt Willow's warm, rough tongue on his face.

"Hi, there, girl." Neil sat up and pulled the little dog into his arms. "Are you fed up, too?"

He looked around. Kate had her back to him and was breathing heavily, deep in sleep. His dad had gone off to Liz's tent ages ago and there was no sign of a policeman on guard. "I reckon we can risk it, girl," he whispered.

He shivered in the cold night air as he crawled out of the sleeping bag. As quietly as he could, he let himself down the tree with Willow scrambling down after him. He had been afraid she would start barking with excitement, but she seemed to understand the need for silence as well as he did.

"Just a quick run, girl," he promised. "And then straight back up the tree, OK?"

Willow looked up at him as if she understood and trotted off to investigate the bushes. Neil stretched his cramped limbs, yawned, and followed her, wishing Jake was with him so they could run and play as they always had. But that was why he was here, he reminded himself, so that Jake and all the other dogs could play safely on the ridgeway, for years and years to come. For that, Neil reckoned, he could stand a bit of discomfort.

The sun was shining brightly as Neil opened his eyes next morning. Not remembering properly where he was, he tried to sit up and felt a hand on his shoulder.

Kate's voice said, "Careful. Don't fall over the edge."

Neil groped his way out of the sleeping bag and sat with his legs dangling over the side of the platform. He ached all over, his eyes were sticky, and he felt as if bits of twig had got inside his clothes. He would have killed for a hot shower.

"Your dad's gone home," Kate went on. She was leaning against the same branch as before, with Willow asleep beside her. "He says he'll see we get some breakfast."

"Good," Neil grunted.

He wasn't looking forward to another day up the tree – or all the days after that. He was stiff and bored and hungry again. And if the weather changed, he would be wet and cold as well. He was beginning to have a clearer idea of what he had taken on, but he still wasn't going to give in.

When Willow woke up he gave her food and water, and the little dog settled down contentedly to sun herself.

Carole appeared later with a flask of hot tea and some bacon sandwiches. Neil expected her to start telling him off again, but she only asked him and Kate how they were feeling.

"I'm really sorry," Kate said. "I know I should be at work. But—"

"That's all right," said Carole. "I understand. And you're not to worry about the kennel work. We're coping."

When she had gone, Neil and Kate shared their breakfast. Neil thought Kate was looking tired, as if she hadn't slept well.

He said, "Kate . . . are you sure you want to stay? Wouldn't you be happier going back to work at King Street?"

Kate wrapped her hands around the plastic mug of tea, and sipped it slowly. "I'd be happier, yes. But being happy isn't always the most important thing. I've got to do this."

"Glen said you could be put in prison or fined."

Kate shrugged.

"Could you afford to pay a fine?" Neil said. He felt that he might be making things worse by talking to Kate about her problems, but he had to try.

"I've been saving up to get married," Kate said.

"But Kate, you can't—"

"Look, Neil," Kate said. He'd never seen her as unhappy as this. "I don't think Glen and I will be getting married. So the money doesn't matter. I'll stick it out here."

She drained her tea, wrapped her arms around her knees, and with a set face stared out into the trees.

At about mid-morning, Neil was roused from an uneasy doze by the sound of footsteps and voices from the direction of the old protest camp on the edge of the wood. He sat up, rubbing his eyes. Willow was sitting erect and let out an excited bark.

A voice Neil didn't recognize called out, "Hi! Anybody there?"

"Over here!" Neil shouted.

"What now?" Kate said.

The footsteps drew nearer. Through the trees came a group of people – two or three men carrying equipment, including a hand-held TV camera, and a young woman wearing jeans and a combat shirt. She looked vaguely familiar to Neil, though he was sure he'd never met her before.

"Hi," she said. "We're an outside broadcast team from North-West TV. We'd like to do an interview for *Polly Presents* – you know, the news magazine programme. I'm Polly."

Now Neil remembered seeing Polly looking out at him from the TV screen. He suddenly felt wildly excited and terrified at the same time. He'd never made a speech on TV before. Nervously he said, "OK. I'm Neil Parker, and this is Kate McGuire and Willow."

"The viewers will love you," Polly said. "I don't think we've ever had a protesting dog before. Will you give me a woof for them, Willow?"

She laughed as Willow barked enthusiastically.

"Right," said Polly. "What I'll do is ask you why you're here and you can say whatever you want to. Keep it short, though."

The TV people started to set up their equipment, while Neil thought through what he would tell the viewers. This was his chance to make a really good public protest about the bypass going across the ridgeway.

While he was thinking, he realized that more people were approaching. A large number of people, by the noise they made; the voices sounded like children.

Polly broke off her conversation with her crew and said, "Cliff, go and see what's going on."

Cliff put his camera down and vanished through the trees. A minute later he came back. "Load of kids," he said. "Looks like a school trip, with a teacher."

"That must be Em's class!" Neil exclaimed. He told Polly, "Emily's my sister. Her class at school have been doing a project on the wildlife of the ridgeway."

Polly's face split into a beaming smile. "That's great! We'll have them in this as well. Cliff, go and ask the teacher, would you? And get her along here with Emily and a couple of the others."

Cliff disappeared again, and when he returned, Mrs Rowntree, Emily's class teacher, was with him, along with Emily, Julie and Toby.

Mrs Rowntree shook hands with Polly. "I'm very pleased to meet you," she said. "We saw your van in the lane on our way up here. What would you like us to do?"

Before Neil knew it, Polly had organized everyone and the camera was rolling. Polly introduced the item and then held out her microphone to Mrs Rowntree.

"Tell me, what is it about this area that makes it so important?"

"The wildlife," Mrs Rowntree said confidently.

"Now that so many children live in cities, it's important for them to have access to open spaces. Up here they can study trees and flowers and animal life."

"Neil, would you agree with that?" Polly asked. She climbed part way up the tree so she could hold the microphone for Neil to speak.

"It's not just for study," Neil said. He glanced at Mrs Rowntree. "That's important, but – it's somewhere we can come with dogs, and let them run free, and get away from all the noise and pollution. This place is special. Building a road will make it just like everywhere else."

"And I bet Willow agrees with that," said Polly. She held the microphone in front of Willow's nose. Neil hoped Willow wouldn't think it was a funny kind of dog treat. "Have you a message for our viewers, Willow?"

Willow let out a loud bark, just as if she was making her own protest.

"You can't argue with that," said Polly. "And if the people of Compton feel as strongly as these plucky protesters, the council can expect more trouble to come. Polly Prescott, for North-West Television, on Compton ridgeway."

*

When the TV crew had packed up and gone, Emily came to talk to Neil.

"That was ace!" she said. "Everybody will see it." She fished in her pocket and pulled out a bag of sweets. "I brought you these."

"Thanks, Em." Neil caught the bag Emily threw up to him. "How's Jake?"

"He's fine. I'll bring him up to see you after school." She glanced over her shoulder as Mrs Rowntree started calling her class to order. "I'll have to go now."

Neil sat and watched as the class gathered around Mrs Rowntree and then scattered through the wood, with their clipboards at the ready. Neil knew, because Emily had told him about a hundred times, that they were comparing this survey with one they had done on the plants and flowers of the ridgeway the term before.

Emily and Julie were carefully examining the ground under Neil's tree. Suddenly Emily stared at something in the grass.

"I haven't seen one of these before," she said. "Let me look it up."

Neil peered down from the platform as she thumbed through the pages of her field guide. Eventually, she found the right page and carefully compared the photograph in the book with the flower in front of her. "It can't be!" she exclaimed.

Julie said, "What's the matter? What is it?"

Emily pointed at the page and then pushed the book under Julie's nose. Wild with curiosity by now, Neil called out, "Em? What have you found?"

Emily didn't reply. In a very quiet voice she said to Julie, "Go and fetch Mrs Rowntree. Don't tell any of the others. We don't want everybody trampling all over it."

Julie got up and went without a word. Neil

thought she almost looked scared. He called out again, "Em!"

Emily raised her head. Her face was pink with excitement and her eyes were shining. "Hang on, Neil," she said. "I don't know if I'm right yet. Wait till I'm sure."

Neil waited, fizzing with impatience, until he heard footsteps approaching through the trees yet again. Then he stiffened. The newcomer wasn't Mrs Rowntree. It was Mr Tyler, the council's chief transport engineer. Constable Grey was following him a few paces behind.

"Oh, no, not him *again!*" Neil said. Willow peered over the edge of the platform and let out a disapproving bark.

"Right, you kids," Mr Tyler said aggressively. "Clear off, will you? The council has sent me up here to fence off this site, ready for the bulldozers."

"We're not doing any harm," Emily said, standing up to face him.

"Just do as you're told," said Mr Tyler. "And you," he added, looking up at Neil. "I might have guessed you would be making trouble."

"I'm not coming down!" Neil retorted. "You can't cut the tree down while we're up here."

"If I was your dad, I'd—"

Neil never found out what Mr Tyler would have done to him, because just then Julie came back with Mrs Rowntree. The teacher was saying, "Don't get your hopes up. There are all kinds of—"

She stopped speaking as she saw Mr Tyler and Constable Grey, and then ignored them again as Emily pointed to the ground in front of her. Slowly she squatted down and examined Emily's find, comparing it carefully with her reference book.

Solemnly she said, "Emily Parker, I think that is a Lady's Slipper Orchid. It's the rarest wild flower in the whole country. There's only one site where it's known to grow wild. And you've found another here, on Compton ridgeway."

Emily went redder still and gave an excited little wriggle. "I thought it was but I just couldn't believe it!"

Mrs Rowntree stood up, pulled a small camera out of her pocket and took several shots of the flower. Neil felt frustrated that he couldn't see it.

"Shouldn't we tell somebody it's here?" Emily suggested. "If it's that important?"

"Of course," said Mrs Rowntree. "The Lady's

Slipper Orchid is protected by law. It's forbidden to pick it or uproot it. This site will have to be *very* carefully preserved."

"Preserved!" Neil exclaimed. He started to stand up and nearly fell off the edge of the platform. "Hey, does that mean they can't build the road?"

Mrs Rowntree swung round towards him. "It certainly does. Nobody—"

"Now just a minute!" Mr Tyler interrupted. "You're not telling me that the council can't do what it likes on its own land. Just for a flower?"

"That's exactly what I'm telling you," said Mrs Rowntree. Neil thought she was enjoying herself. "Nobody is allowed to interfere with this site. Looking after this new specimen – and any others there might be – is more important than anything else. That's the law."

"Brilliant!" said Emily, with a beaming smile.

Neil felt his face split into a smile, too. So many people had been telling him that unpleasant things were the law. It was good to hear that the law would protect the ridgeway too for the sake of a flower.

Mr Tyler's face slowly turned red. He looked furious. He took a step towards the flower, one hand held out as if he was going to pull it up.

Emily pushed herself in front of him. "Don't even think about it."

Constable Grey moved up to stand beside the transport engineer. "I wouldn't try it, sir," he said.

Mr Tyler made a furious snorting noise. "This is crazy. And so are all of you!" he shouted as he stormed off. "The council will be hearing about this!"

"Yes, they will!" Neil yelled after him. "We'll tell them to put the road somewhere else!"

He burst out laughing as the transport engineer disappeared, and Willow barked loudly.

"And another thing," Mrs Rowntree said when she could make herself heard. "This means that you, young man, can come down from there right now."

Chapter Ten

Neil didn't need telling twice. He slithered down the trunk of the tree; Willow skidded down after him, still barking excitedly.

"Be careful!" Emily said. "Don't put your great feet on it!"

Neil crouched down to look at the Lady's Slipper Orchid. It was just starting to come out, on a single stem with narrow leaves. Its petals were a purplish colour, unfolding from a yellow centre. He'd never seen anything like it, but even so he was surprised that one small flower could cause as much fuss as this.

"It's really that important?" he asked Mrs Rowntree.

"It really is," she said.

Kate had followed him down from the platform, and captured Willow. Holding the little dog under her arm, she too came to look at the flower.

"Kate," said Mrs Rowntree, "will you do something for me, please?"

"Sure."

"Stay here and keep an eye on this, while I round up the class. Neil, you'd better stay too. Emily and Julie, come with me. We'll go back to school and tell Mr Hamley. He'll know what to do next."

When the others had gone Kate sat on the ground next to the flower, while Neil threw a stick for Willow to chase and get some of the exercise she badly needed. He was careful *not* to throw it near the orchid. The white dog bobbed up and down through the undergrowth, barking happily.

When she brought the stick back for Neil he threw it again, just as a figure walked through the trees into the clearing. The stick fell at Glen's feet.

"Hi," he said. As Willow bounced up to fetch the stick, he ruffled her short curly coat. "Hello, Willow. You all came down from the tree, then."

Kate stood up. "Yes. Emily found a rare flower." She sounded awkward, as if she was talking to a stranger. "It should mean they won't be able to build the road through here."

Glen went over and looked at the flower. "That's great," he said. He didn't sound as if the flower was what he wanted to talk about. "Kate," he went on. "It's all my fault. I'm really sorry. Can't we . . . well, can't we try again?"

Kate said nothing, but Neil saw her brush a tear away. A minute later, Glen was hugging her.

Neil looked at Willow. "If you ask me," he said, "it's a good thing we're here to guard the flower."

At King Street, the doors of Red's Barn were flung wide open. Sunshine fell on long trestle tables covered with white cloths and tray after tray of delicious-looking snacks and sandwiches, arranged around a magnificent wedding cake. Pots of wild flowers decorated the tables and ledges around the walls.

"But no Lady's Slippers!" said Emily to Neil, laughing. "We're not allowed to pick those!"

Kate and Glen had been married that morning in Compton Parish Church and now all their guests had come to King Street for the wedding reception. The barn was crowded. Guests spilled out on to the grass around the rescue centre.

Neil could see Dr Harvey with his dogs Finn and Sandy, Mike Turner, Gavin Thorpe the vicar with his Labrador Jet, and loads of other friends of King Street Kennels who wanted to wish Kate and Glen good luck on their special day.

"Let's get some food," he said to Emily. "I'm starving."

As he wriggled his way between the guests towards the tables, he came across his mother talking to Jane Hammond. Neil couldn't get over how elegant Carole looked in the new blue dress she had bought for the wedding. It was nothing like the sweaters and jeans she wore to work with the dogs.

"Here are Neil and Emily now," she said to Jane. "I think you two will want to hear this."

"There was a council meeting yesterday," said Jane, smiling. "George Marbeck told the action group all about it. And they've voted to make the whole of the ridgeway a conservation area."

"Yes!" Neil sprang up and punched the air.

Several guests looked round to see what was making him so excited.

"The new bypass will be built along the other route," Jane added. "And the council are looking into ways to protect the Lady's Slippers."

"And we can go on walking the dogs up there for ever and ever," said Emily happily.

"How did Mr Jepson vote at the meeting?" Neil asked curiously.

"George said the vote was unanimous, so he must have voted along with everybody else."

Neil grinned quietly. It was just too bad for Happydale Health Farm, but he didn't see any point in talking about it now. Mr Jepson's secret was safe at last!

He said goodbye to Jane and worked his way over to the tables where he piled up a plate with sandwiches and sausage rolls and slices of quiche. His father, who was running the bar, poured glasses of orange juice for him and Emily.

They took their loaded plates outside again, and Neil collected Jake from Bev, who had been looking after him while Neil and Emily fetched something to eat.

"You'll need to give him a good long run when

this is over," Bev said as Neil settled down on the grass and made Jake sit beside him.

"Sure will," said Neil.

"All the way up the ridgeway!" said Emily.

As they were eating, Neil looked around to see still more friends. His Uncle Jack and Aunt Mary were chatting to Sergeant Moorhead, while his cousin Steve tried to persuade his crazy Labrador, Ricky, not to roll on the grass in front of the well-behaved Sherlock.

Emily nudged Neil. "Look at Dotty!"

Neil laughed. Dotty the Dalmatian had wound her lead round Mr Hamley's legs as she tried to play with her son Scrap, Toby Sparrow's puppy. Mr Hamley was trying to unwind her and juggle a glass of wine, and at the same time make polite conversation with Mrs Sparrow.

The sun was shining and nothing was missing to make the day as good as it could possibly be.

Not far from the doors of the barn, Kate and Glen were standing having their photograph taken. Jake kept trying to join in.

"I don't think I've ever seen Glen in a suit before," said Neil. "He looks really smart."

"I think Kate looks beautiful," said Emily.

Neil grunted. He supposed that Kate's white

wedding dress was pretty special, but he preferred her in the jeans and bright jumpers she wore for her kennel work. She looked very happy.

Sarah came skipping by, twirling in her long bridesmaid's frock; Mr McGuire, Kate's dad, called her and Emily to be photographed. Neil whistled for Jake and gave him a piece of sausage roll. He heard the sound of a car drawing up in the drive, and a late-arriving guest came through the gate. It was Liz Hart, with Willow on a lead.

When she saw Kate and Glen, who were just relaxing after the photographs were finished, she hurried over and hugged both of them.

"Congratulations!" she said. "I hope you'll be really happy."

"You've heard about the road?" said Glen.

"Yes, isn't it brilliant? And did you see Willow on TV? She was brilliant, too – and you Neil," Liz added, seeing Neil close by. "I bet you got more public support from that one interview than we did from our whole protest."

Feeling embarrassed, Neil muttered his thanks. "What happened to you?" he asked. "Are you still in trouble with the police?"

Liz shook her head. "No, thanks to your Sergeant Moorhead. A policeman who didn't sympathize with us could have made it a lot nastier. Anyway, it's all over now. Mr Tyler withdrew his complaint against Willow once he realized it wouldn't do him any good, so we don't have to worry any more." Laughing, she added, "I can't stop thinking that we were camped up there right next to that orchid, and none of us ever noticed it! Emily, you should be really proud of yourself."

Emily went red. "It was just lucky that I saw it."

"So what's next, Liz?" Glen asked. "Are you staying round here?"

"No, I'm off to France," said Liz. "A French group has asked for advice on protesting about some development near their end of the Channel Tunnel. I could be over there for months." She hesitated and then went on, "That's one reason I came. I can't take Willow with me, or if I did she'd have to go into quarantine when I come back. And besides, I'm not sure that the sort of life I lead is really the best one for a dog. So I thought I'd ask you if you would like to have her." She grinned at Glen's surprised expression. "As a wedding present."

"Well . . . what do you think?" Glen asked Kate.

Kate had already stooped over to scratch Willow behind the ears and run her fingers through the dog's rough coat. "I think she's the best wedding present anyone could ever give us! Thank you, Liz. I promise we'll take good care of her."

"And if you need any help with her," Neil said, "you know where to find the Puppy Patrol!"

Glen glanced at his watch. "Well, Mrs Paget," he said to Kate, "it's time we were getting changed. We've got to drive to the Lake District. I suppose I'd better ring the hotel and make sure it's OK to bring Willow with us."

"That's where you're going?" said Neil. "The Lake District?"

"Yes," Kate said. "For a week. Why?"

"Oh, nothing," Neil said, grinning. "Only now that you've got Willow, I just hope there'll be plenty of trees!"